THE HAUNTING OF THE PARANORMAL ROMANCE AWARDS

CHRISTOPH PAUL
MANDY DE SANDRA

CL4SH

Copyright © 2020 Christoph Paul & Mandy De Sandra

Cover by Dyer Wilk

CLASH Books

clashbooks.com

All rights reserved.

ISBN: 978-1-944866-80-8

DEDICATION

*Christoph: To the memory of my mother,
you would have liked this book, mom.*

*Mandy: To all my homegirls and
philosophy qweens—
Y'all give me life.*

INTRODUCTION

There's nothing more horrifying than being stuck in a room with a group of women that either love or hate you. My fans sit in the audience, hanging onto every word I say, the way most guys at the bar pretend to. A few of them are even wearing t-shirts of my book covers. My book covers aren't very flattering.

A lot of these women flew across country to attend The Haunted Heart Conference. I am surrounded by people who adore me, but of course all I can focus on are the hateful petty bitches sitting next to me.

The way too bright lights it the Sheraton Office Room keep reflecting off our plastic nametags with the little haunted hearts above our names. Beside me is the host, Alexandra Newton, or Dr. Alexandra, who has to mention her PhD every 5 minutes. So we all call her PhD.

Nora Carpenter sits there with her smug and perfectly contoured face. She tries to look like she's not wearing makeup, but bitch, you are wearing a ton of make up, and you need to stop it with the Avon lady smiles.

I'm still pissed about the backhanded shade she Tweeted: *.@AutumnCollins is the only author nominated* *this year who is self-published and doesn't even have a high school degree. #Inspiration #HHAwards*

Bitch.

I haven't hated a woman this much since my mother and my rehab counselor.

The other nominees for the Haunted Heart Award — Christine Phenomenon and Angie Foxx don't hate me like Nora does, but they do not like me either. And then there is Shira Constantine, who is too crazy to hate anyone. She hasn't said a word since the panel started, but keeps playing with her rosary beads.

We were told to dress business casual for the panel, but Shira came in wearing a black nightgown and mourning veil, looking like a gothic lunch lady. Shira is probably taking a nap behind that damn thing, but the sad truth is we'll probably all lose to her.

PhD continues to talk about the history of paranormal romance. I tuned out when she mentioned Dante.

Her Dante tangent finally ends and she says, "Alright, that's enough of me. Let's open it up for questions," she points at woman with a bad perm and a purple pant suit.

The woman nervously smiles at all of us. "Oh my god, I can't believe I'm talking to all of you. I'm such a fan of... almost all of you...my name's Clara by the way...oh you can see my name tag...sorry...Ok...so like all the paranormal romance reading I am doing has inspired me to write stories of my own...and, little by little, it has added up, and I have finished my first novel and I don't know what to do next. Should I self-publish?"

Before I can tell her the benefits and the awfulness of self-pubbing, Nora answers, "Carla, come on, we all know that self-published books are mostly garbage." Nora looks at me. "No offense, Autumn." She looks back at the small crowd. "Jesus, ladies, what's with your generation? No patience. You have to be patient—that's being a professional. Professionals have agents, editors, and publishers—people who tell you if it's shit or fertilizer that a great editor and publisher can grow flowers out of..." she looks back at me and gives that same fake af smile. "My fellow nominee, Autumn, is an anomaly. You know what that words means, right, Autumn?"

"Yes," I grit through my teeth and force out a fake smile to match hers.

The other nominees ignore the comments, reluctant to pick a side, but PhD says, "I have to agree with Nora to an extent, but I have only worked with university presses, do you have another view Autumn?"

I nod and feel déjà vu about being stuck in a room with women who hate each other while being forced to be honest about who they are. I really thought I had left that behind in rehab.

"Yeah, I hear this a lot," I say defensively. "Like, I learned in the program, all I can share is my experience, strength, and hope...Basically, I got lucky. I didn't even really write fiction til a couple years ago, and it was story-telling more than writing that found me. Many of you know this, and some of you don't but I sobered up at the Ashland Treatment Center for Women and I hated it there and so did the other women. One night to pass the time, I began telling a ghost story. It was a love story as well. It was like I was possessed. The story just came out of me. A meth addict recorded it on her phone, and then every night after our AA meetings I would continue the story. It felt really good to connect with the other women with my words. By the time I was done with treatment, I was 90 days sober and I had a novel.

"My sponsor told me to get a job and I wasn't qualified for anything that would pay the bills that had been piling up. I heard about KDP and self-publishing and tran-scribed the story I told in rehab. It paid my bills for the next year and then I just kept writing and here I am, but..."

I pause remembering there are some truths you don't ever share with the group.

"But what?" Nora prods, "I am even drinking your Kool-Aid, maybe I am doing this all wrong."

"But, Carla...I can't tell you what to do, it just comes down to you doing what feels right."

Nora rolls her eyes, "Send it to an agent, or develop a drinking problem."

Twenty different women scramble to grab their phones to spill the latest #ParaShade tea. It's a pretty good hashtag about the rivalry between Nora and me, but it hasn't helped sell my books.

PhD smiles and says, "This is way more fun than academic conferences. Let's move on and focus on the genre itself and what defines a great paranormal romance book..."

PhD is cut off when Shira slams her fist on the table. "Lies and blasphemy! No more lies and disrespect to the spirits! I do not write fiction!"

Nora laughs sardonically, "Here we go," while gasps and looks of bafflement come out of the audience but Shira's fans clap and laugh. I've seen some YouTube videos of Shira's meltdowns. This should be good.

"Silence!" Shira commands.

She's breathing so heavily that the black veil goes up and down like it's haunted by a hyperventilating ghost.

Shira cracks her knuckles and continues, "I am the only *true* paranormal romance author here! I know its truth and the rest of these writers are selling lies. My memoir, *My Husband Never Left* is the only real paranormal romance book nominated for the award. Because it is true! And if it does not win, the spirits, including my deceased husband will be very, very angry. Do what is right, but do what thou wilt."

Shira returns to sitting in silence behind her veil.

The live tweeters type with glee, especially those wearing Shira's *Spirit Squad* Shirts. I try to peer behind Shira's veil. I can't tell if she is serious or if this is just a brilliant persona. Whatever it is, I wish I had what she has. Not her writing ability, though it's definitely better than mine, but her book sales and specifically her agent, Janet Rose—the best agent out there. Maybe Janet told her to do this persona, if so, it is working perfectly.

I try to spot Janet in the audience for the thirtieth time. I pretend to stretch so I can look over the heads over the big haired women in the front, but I can't find her anywhere. I crane my neck out to see the back row, but no Janet.

A woman Cosplaying as one of my characters, Madame Noire, wearing her trademark top hat, gets up to go to the bathroom and seated behind her I see him. He is tall, black, and has a rugged Idris Elba thing going. He looks familiar. Damn. He looks like boxer that lives in the gym. What the hell is he doing here, and can he please lift his hand up to see if there is a wedding ring on it.

Our eyes meet and his smile expands, I recognize him now— he's a horror guy, he writes some hardcore stuff that sort of crosses over into erotica.

I feel my face go red. Damn, I can feel myself blushing. I'm taken out of my reverie when PhD taps on the table to get the room attention, and says, "Our panel is coming to a close. I want to thank all the nominees. We will now have our signings and I believe Shira is doing a special guided... um meditation or séance. Then the big event, so don't forget to dress up tonight, ladies and gentlemen, this Paranormal Romance Awards is going to be our best one yet!"

CHAPTER ONE

I follow the other nominees out of the conference room and go to the book nook. The Portland Marriott is nice but it smells like a creepy geography teacher I had in high school. The organizer, Tam Rivers, points us to our signing spot. Thankfully, Nora and I are on opposite sides.

Shira follows behind me and surveys her spot. "I will only sit on the right. It's a spiritual thing. Please respect it."

Tam smiles politely at Shira. "Um Shira, your name and books are already set up there. I ... um ... want to respect your spiritual..."

"Move me right! I must always be on the right. You must..."

"Um, I'll switch," I stammer. "It's ok, we can move the books."

Shira doesn't say anything, she just sits in my spot and stares off in either boredom or sorrow, or both.

"Thank you, Autumn, we want our star writers happy," Tam says, switching the signs and restacking the piles of books.

I take a big breath, part passive aggressive and part anxiety and sit next to Nora. She doesn't even acknowledge me and I glance over her larger and more diverse pile. She even has a few of her literary novels, published in the early 2000s before she jumped on the paranormal train. One paperback even has a blurb from The New Yorker. Her covers have a sleek and attractive quality that matches her black business suit attire.

My covers, on the other hand, I'll admit do look better as eBooks which are 90% of my sales...they sell. Well, at least they used to. I printed some off KDP, but I am already regretting it, because the paper and cover quality is clearly inferior to hers.

Nora still doesn't look at me but she glances sideways at my titles. "You know most self-published covers are atrocious but yours are kind of nice, Autumn. Did you have a friend do them for you?"

Damn, she is even better at being passive aggressive than being a bitch. "I got them off Selfpubbookcovers.com. Seventy-five bucks for each, but I get to keep all the royalties. It worked for the first book, so I kept using them."

"Well, good job, that looks like about a hundred to a hundred and twenty five dollar cover," Nora says, smiling and leans her chair back like she has something profound to say. "That is a benefit of doing it yourself, but let me tell you, Autumn, nothing beats getting a five figure and sometimes six figure advance. Having publishers pay for marketing, covers, and even a publicist. Trust me. There is a reason why I don't self-pub."

I want to ask her about advances and specifically about her agent, but even as she leans back she's still looking down on me — like my mother, like my counselor, like every girl snickering at school, at the bar, in life.

"Well, the paperbacks are really just for my fans. Everyone reads eBooks now," I turn my attention to the gathering crowd and smile. "My line is so long, I hope my arm doesn't get too tired. Seeing your line though, you should be ok."

Nora smile-scowls at me as excited readers step forward, our books clutched in their arms.

I'm halfway through signing books, saying the Serenity Prayer over and over again to myself. I'm not a believer in a higher power but since I got sober I say it every morning.It seems to center me. My fanbase is no longer enough to pay off my debts.

One of the women in line is carrying a jack and coke. I can smell it and I remember Mr. 'Tyler Durden" as was his not that clever nickname—my drinking partner/ex-boyfriend. It didn't hurt that he had rich dad and a really good cock. Our last night together we were drinking at our favorite bar in Ashland, Oregon when a pain in my side struck me hard—it hurt so bad that I fell off the barstool.

At the hospital, the fabulous Mr. Durden didn't want to pay the bill, and I was too drunk to have even known about the ACA. After a two-day stay in the hospital, I found out I had cirrhosis of the liver and couldn't drink ever again. Not a drop. And my dear Mr. Durden told me he had to leave and go see his father.

I was pissed, but angrier at myself.

I went to our place and found a note saying I had two weeks to find a new home. I was no longer a hot piece of ass he could get drunk with, and basically he needed more money from daddy and new pussy from Tinder.

I hated laying in our bed.

I hated being sober even more.

I didn't know what to do and I didn't know how the fuck I was going to live. I went on Facebook to beg for help. But midway through my post, by fate or by algorithm, I saw an ad for the Ashland Treatment Center for women. I figured I was already going to be in debt for life because of the hospital bills and medication I had to take that I couldn't afford. I might as well add treatment to my pile of debt and figure out how to do this sobriety thing.

Years later, I am still sober and am in the 1% of writers that actually make over 40k a year and yet I am still in debt. Kindle Unlimited has killed me and if I don't get a big payday I am not even going to be able to afford my shitty apartment.

I need an advance and I need it to be a big one.

The last fan in line hands me a book. I sign it and say, "Thank you so much," for what feels like the hundredth time.

She smiles. "No, *thank you*, but I gotta say Autumn, I keep waiting for a new book from you, but nothing. You used to put them out every three months but it's been almost nine months now."

"I got something big planned. It will be worth the wait, I promise," I lie.

"Cool!" she exclaims with giddiness, and walks away with my third book, *Love's Tyrant*.

I look down at my pile, and half of my books are still there, at least I sold more books than Nora, who is still sitting and typing something on her phone—probably another shitty Tweet about me.

Shira's line is the only one still going, damn, it is not even halfway done. Damn it, she is so going to win that damn award.

The next woman in line screams as she walks up to Shira, "Oh my god, I love your book so much. Easily my favorite of the year, maybe even the decade. I am the blogger of This Lady is Gaga 4 Dark Romance and I would love to interview you!"

"No," Shira hisses behind her black veil, "You 'bloggers' spread lies, saying my story is not true. Labeling it fiction! It is my life and the spirits still speak to me."

"Oh no, Shira," the woman gasps defensively. "Your book is true to me. It is real. I swear."

"Very well, as long as you respect my *true* paranormal romance about my deceased husband, I will answer your questions. Talk to my agent Janet Rose, she will be speaking later today, she'll set it up."

Nora is done typing whatever she was typing and says, "She is my agent too. She gets things done. Janet is the best."

"She is my agent too, she'll hook you up," says a deep, masculine voice.

I look up and see Mr. Tall Dark and Handsome staring down at me. He slaps down a worn-out copy of my book *The Gargoyle and The Gentleman*. "Wanna sign this and then grab some lunch?"

CHAPTER TWO

THE BAR LIGHTS ARE A LITTLE TOO BRIGHT AND I'M stumbling over words, sharing space with this 6'4 hot as hell *hunk*—I've never used that word without irony, but that's what I think when I look at Wrath. I've been sober long enough to hang in a bar and not feel the urge, but I can't remember being sober on a date where I was so attracted to the guy.

A waitress comes over again and Wrath smiles at her but she only looks at me. Her hair is up in a tight bun. She looks like she's in her mid-twenties. The dark circles under her eyes give her a haunted look. "Food will be coming soon..." she pauses, like she's not sure what to say next but adds shyly, "I'm sorry Miss Collins, my manager said we shouldn't bother the guests, but...I'm just such a huge fan. I'm Tonya by the way...and reading your books on my iPad after work, when my boyfriend hangs with his friends... I just really love your stories and your characters."

"Aw thank you," I say, and I truly mean it.

Wrath smiles, showing off his perfect teeth. "She is really good, right?"

"Super good. Autumn, you and Shira are my favorite writers right now," she says, smiling.

Wrath stretches his long frame, his leg brushing up against mine and asks her, "What do you think of Missy Rapture?"

"She is a great writer, but I just don't get into her stories. I feel like she doesn't really understand women."

Wrath blushes and slides his leg away from mine. "Fair enough. I think she's got a lot of growing to do still."

"Probably," the waitress says, looking back at me, "I gotta get back, but I just *had* to tell you how much I love your books."

She walks back toward the kitchen. I loved feeling Wrath's leg against mine. I brush against his knee. "So, you are Missy Rapture, aren't you? You're taller than I thought."

"Damn," Wrath said shaking his head, laughing. "What gave it away?"

"I could read it on your face."

He blushes again.

"It makes sense now why a horror author is here."

"Oooh, you recognized me too."

"I don't read much horror, but I saw a book of yours on an erotica blog when they did a horror month."

"I see, I see," he says. "What about Missy Rapture? Do you read 'her' work?"

I laugh and scrunch up my face in embarrassment, "Sorry, I haven't heard of her."

"Ouch."

"Sorry, who are you published with?"

Wrath smirks and said, "Nobody. I'm like you, I self-publish in this genre, but I'm really here to see my agent. I think she keeps me on her roster just to show she represents black people, but she still gets me a decent tie-in-novel here and there. "

I want to forget about business, I want to enjoy this date but the thought of Janet makes me anxious again. I miss when I just could just drink away these nerves and forget everything.

"What is it?" Wrath asks. "You're not very good at hiding what you feel either. Something I said?"

I take a big sip of my coffee and set it down. "No...I mean yeah...it's the publishing stuff. You mentioning your agent...I'm dealing with some career crossroads and it is driving me a little crazy."

Wrath nods thoughtfully. "I feel ya. I do the horror film tie-in novels that Janet gets, and then self-publish paranormal romance stuff like you. The novel tie-ins pay my rent for the year and keep me from having to teach high school."

I hate asking for help especially with the first datable guy I've met since leaving rehab. I'm trying to find the words to ask him help me talk to his agent, but for the first time his eyes aren't focusing on me.

He points over my head and says, "You gotta turn around! Look who it is, you won't believe it."

I turn around and see someone who is unmistakably Fabio. Wow, Fabio must be the surprise guest that I've been hearing about. He's smiling and waving at people taking pictures on their smartphones.

"Yo Fabio! You still look good, man," Wrath calls out.

Fabio nods and snaps his finger at us before vanishing into the hotel elevator.

"I can't believe it, that's freaking Fabio! I'm older than you and you might not remember them, but I loved those butter commercials."

It's kind of endearing how excited he's getting about Fabio.

I feel his leg against mine again.

"I mean he's pretty special, he's Fabio," I say. "You're pretty hot, but this could be my only shot with Fabio."

He laughs. "Ah, I see how it is, it's that hair, isn't it. Man, I lost mine in my twenties. I don't have those Fabio genes."

"Yeah, what I can say, Fabio has some sexy hair."

"Yeah, yeah, I bet you that's not even his real hair, it's probably a wig," he says, leaning in. I can smell his cologne mixing with his sweat. It's intoxicating.

I smile back and say, "Or he made a deal with the devil to keep that gorgeous hair."

The crumbs of the chocolate cake we just shared are the only things remaining on the table. Tonya comes over and drops off the check. "No rush, I can see you're having fun...you guys look really cute together. I hope it inspires a new book."

She winks and walks away. I laugh and blush, and Wrath says, "She's getting a good ass tip."

I reach for the check but he takes out his wallet. "Sorry, I'm old school. I got it."

"And they say chivalry is dead!" I say, giggling like an idiot.

"I'm one in a million. I coulda told you that," he says, sliding his credit card into the check holder.

"So, do you have any panels before dinner?" I ask, picturing us soaking in the hotel hot tub.

"Yeah, I gotta do a movie-tie in panel in like two hours, what about you?"

"I finally have some free time."

Wrath nodded and said, "So...you wanna hang for a little more..."

"I do, it's just ...wait, is this like a thing you do? Macking on paranormal romance writers at Cons?"

His leg knocks against mine and I knock him back, ""Nah, most of y'all are too crazy for me."

"Damn."

"I'm just playing."

"I know, but..." I stop as I feel his hand grab mine. So this is what it feels like to be super into someone when you're sober.

"But what?" he asks holding my hand.

"But, I...I didn't come here for this. I came for business stuff. It's...damn it, sorry...It was way easier to talk to dudes when I was a drunk."

Wrath squeezes tighter, tight enough to make me feel safe. "Hey, it's alright. I know how it is in the business and I know the loneliness. I recently got divorced. I get it. This is new for me too."

"That sucks. How long ago?"

"Nine months ago. And it does suck, it sucks really bad. A lot of times she would come here with me, but..."

I see sadness in his soulful brown eyes. Seeing that softness in him makes me just want him more.

"It's ok. If it makes you feel better, your recent divorce somehow just made you a little hotter."

"Ha, thanks. I haven't really dated either, but then I saw *you*."

"I've barely had time go on dates. I didn't realize that writing and publishing your own stuff is like 60-hour job, and I got to go to a meeting at least every other day...it's hard and it's..."

"Lonely," Wrath says, nodding his head. "Then you're editing or teaching online to writers who can't write...it's a grind and it's harder to do it while going through a divorce."

I think of all the shit I'll return home to: the lonely one bedroom apartment full of medication and hospital bills that keep me close to broke, and the voice files...those fucking voice files of stories that go nowhere. No new books, no new money. Maybe I need to get laid to get real inspiration, or is this an excuse to con-slut it up? Does it even matter?

I go in for a kiss.

He kisses me back and I don't care if there are people taking Twitter photos of us right now. This feels really right.

His lips are like how liquor tastes in my dreams.

I stop kissing.

"You said, you had an hour?"

Wrath nods and says, "Actually, I got two."

CHAPTER THREE

WE REACH MY HOTEL ROOM AND MY HAND IS SHAKING while I slide my card in the door. It clicks open and out of habit I look toward the liquor cabinet. I'm as turned on as I am nervous.

He looks nervous too.

"You never cheated? You know, on her?" I ask him.

"Nah, that's just not me."

"You're better than me."

He kisses me and puts his arms around my waist. He's a good foot taller than me. I stand on tiptoes and whisper. "I want you."

I slide out of my dress and he lifts off his shirt.

He slips off his jeans and damn...he's already hard and it's looking really crowded in those boxers.

I take a deep breath and take off my underwear. Naked. So naked right now and I didn't shave. I forgot how good it feels to feel sexy and desired by someone.

He picks me up and takes me to the bed. When he lays me down, I hear something popping and crinkling under my ass.

"Oh shit," I yelp and jump.

I reach under my ass and fish out a half eaten bag of orange Cheetos.

"I do like that Cheeto flavor," he says.

"I hope I don't taste like Cheetos, now. I don't want a Cheeto pussy."

We both laugh.

I feel nervous. I always do when guys go down on me the first time, but damn, he's good.

He puts his fingers inside of me while licking my clit. I can't remember being with a guy who really knew his way around a woman's body. Maybe I should have dated guys in their forties sooner, but the ones like Wrath were usually taken.

I've written so many hot sex scenes, but I've never really lived any until this moment.

I get down on all fours, crawling over to him as he lays down. He is hard. I start sliding his cock into my mouth, slowly at first, easing my way down as I hold back my gag reflex and pray I can make it all the way down without hurling the cake I just ate.

I don't know if I ever actually 69ed sober. I loosen my jaw and sink down into it, my eyes watering, my pussy getting that warm tingly feeling.

I'm waiting for him to taste me again but he starts giggling and my stomach clenches. "What...what's wrong?"

"Um...you got a Cheeto on your perineum...the taint...the..."

"I know what it is," I say mortified, and unable to move.

"Do you want me to get it off?"

"Yes!"

I feel his lips and hear a crunch. He says, "I told you I like that flavor."

We laugh hysterically. I turn around and touch his face. "You're really something, you know?"

"So are you, Autumn."

I back and feel nervous, realizing this could actually be meaningful sex for once.

I am resting in the crook between Wrath's shoulder and chest as he smokes a cigarette. "That was... something else."

"Yeah ..." he says, sounding almost stoned. "I don't have words right now for what that was."

Out of habit I want a drag, I reach for the cigarette and drink on the nightstand. I read in the Huffington Post that orgasms are supposed to relax me. And it has, until reality comes creeping back.

"You want one."

"Yes, but no...I can't smoke. Health stuff."

He nods thoughtfully and I feel heaven drifting way and reality fully re-materializing. What now? I feel all the knots returning, thinking about going back down to the Con and dealing with the other women.

"Man, I'm cum stoned, but I feel...I feel you starting to have panic vibes," Wrath says. "Talk to me."

Damn it, he's sensitive and empathic while still being super hot. I just fucked a damn unicorn.

"I didn't plan to meet somebody at a paranormal romance conference. I'm definitely not here for this," I say awkwardly.

"Me neither, but it happened. And I'm glad it did. And I would not mind it happening again."

"Really?"

"Hells yeah."

"Me too."

"Why did you come?" I ask. "You are not even selling books."

"It's the only time my agent will meet and talk business with me. She won't Skype. And I can only tell when she's bullshitting me by looking at her face. Are you here just in case you win the award?"

I playfully slap his ass, "Thanks for the vote of confidence. No, I know Shira's winning that. I'm not here for the awards...I'm actually here to talk your agent.

"Why? You must be making bank self-pubbing."

"Kindle Unlimited, a crowded market, writer's block, and a lot of bills and debts are keeping me quite bankless."

"Damn, but yeah, it's the advances that keep the lights on. You try Patreon?"

"I can't do it. I just can't do that. I can't ..."

"I get it, you struggle to ask for help and you got writer's block."

"Pretty much."

"Well shit, girl, you just need an advance and agent to get you on track. Why didn't you tell me before, I can hook you up with a meeting."

"Really?"

"Yeah, you don't have to act all shameful," Wrath says with a chuckle.

"It's embarrassing."

He nods and says, "Shit, I've been there. Debt. Bad debt. I can't front, it definitely didn't help my marriage. But when the debt went away and we still had problems, I knew we were fucking done. The writer life, it's hard."

"So fucking hard."

"But you are right to seek my agent," he adds, and I see a twinkle of gratitude pop up in his eyes. "Janet saved my ass and made me some good money. Seriously. She gets you hooked up. She got me the right editor, the right gig, and the right writing partner—that is what got me out of a bad writer's block. With your sales, she can get you a good six figure advance."

"That is what I need! Unfortunately, I heard that she thinks my books are crap."

Wrath laughs and shakes his head. He looks a little embarrassed, "She thought the same of mine, but the she saw that I could make her money. I became her token brother to write horror movie tie-in novelizations."

"That's what I keep hearing in the writer groups on Facebook. That, and how much Nora thinks I suck."

"Whatever with her, she just thinks she is above us genre folk, even though that is where she made her real money."

"I hate women, they're all bitches, except for when they read my books."

"I am a fan, not of bitches, but it's good to have a bitch for an agent," he says and reaches for over to grab his phone.

"You're not into post-fuck selfies are you?...that's kind of... icky."

"I'm forty, come on," he says shaking his head and starts typing something on his iPhone. He presses send and I hear the swoosh as he places it back on the counter.

"What did you send?"

"Kiss me and I'll tell you."

"Seriously, what did you send?"

He stays silent but I see a little smirk. God, those lips. "You don't have to blackmail me to do that," I say and give him a long kiss.

I forget about everything until the phone vibrates and falls off the nightstand.

Wrath reaches down and grabs and his phone. "It's a text from Janet."

"Let me see!"
He clicks on her name and we read it together.

U r fucking her, aren't u?
Fine, have her meet me at 3 in the courtyard.

CHAPTER FOUR

I walk outside to the courtyard. There is a new confidence in my step. I can smell him on me and I feel my shoulders arch back, but they quickly slump to their usual position when I see Shira standing next to Janet Rose.

Behind them a group of fangirls wearing Shira shirts sit cross-legged in front of strategically placed witchy looking esoteric symbols—they are silver and look like they were bought from JoAnn's and cut by an eight year old.

Janet sees me and beckons. "Autumn, please join us. You can observe or participate in um...Shira's workshop."

"It is not a workshop!" Shira exclaims, exasperated.

She lifts a golden trophy with a demonic vampirish looking man's face inside of a heart. "This is a séance for the spirits to bless the award, and for my great love's return."

Jesus, if they are letting her bless the award, they must really think she is a shoe-in to win. She looks insane holding the award up like she is freaking Harry Potter and it's her wand.

Poor girl, I guess she really did lose it when her

husband passed. I feel bad for her, I met women in rehab like her who had lost everyone and everything, and I knew they'd never get better. They were just, broken.

"Um, I can come back, after this," I tell Janet.

"Nonsense," Janet says with her infamous fake smile. "Come and witness Shira's workshhh.... I mean, séance."

The women start clapping and cheering making fake ghost sounds.

"Silence, fools! Don't disrespect the spirits!" Shira screams.

"Join me over here, Autumn," Janet calls me over.

"She can watch but she cannot participate," Shira orders. "Paranormal Romance posers cannot participate in this ritual."

"Um...ok, both counts," I say, walking towards Janet.

Shira lifts the award high in air. "Gaze upon the power." Some of the women look like they're trying to hold in their laughter, but others are totally going along with it. Their eyes barely blinking, like they're being zombified.

The sun reflects off the silver symbols. I feel a type of heat reflecting off them.

Damn, she's got a really good marketing shtick.

It almost feels real.

A middle aged woman in the crowd with red bangs raises her hand and asks, "Shira, what do these symbols mean? Are they Egyptian?"

"No, you fool. These are the symbols my husband and spirit friends told me to bring."

The woman nods in amazement and says, "Wow."

"Wow is right," Shira answers back. "Now each of you lift up the ancient language of the spirits and hold them high."

The women follow Shira's commands and awkwardly hold up the silver symbols.

I turn away and whisper to Janet. "I gotta ask, is she for real?"

Janet stares at Shira positioning the women into a circle. "You tell me."

For the first time, maybe ever, I see Shira smile. "Yes, hold them and repeat after me: Alû, abadu, benala, Alû."

Shira walks into the middle of the circle and waves the Haunted Heart Award over their symbols and their bodies.

"What the fuck?!" I laugh.

"Silence, or the spirits won't come!" Shira wails at me and pauses, scowling, until I stop laughing.

Janet waves her finger in front of my face and says, "She is new to your world, Shira. Please, carry on, this is very beautiful."

Shira returns her attention to her captive audience. She walks through the circle, tracing the sign of the magical symbols across their faces and their bodies.

"Now tell the spirits what you want. For when I win tonight, they will bless you, and they will be freed from their torture." She turns to us and says, "Even you must open your hearts to the spirits."

Janet stares me down until I follow her into the circle.

Shira hands the award to a woman wearing an *Original Sinners* T-Shirt. She is in her mid-thirties, ecstatically smiling. "Um, hey. I'm Tonya and my main desire is to ugh...like...I just want my husband to act out some scenes like in the books. Even though he's alive, the ghosts I read about in your book have the kind of passion I wish he had..."

"Bless us her, Alû! Bless her!" Shira chants.

I watch the award being passed around like a spirit stick, from woman to woman, and hear cries for hotter sex and more money or meeting weight goals.

I am at least getting hot sex now, thanks to whatever it

is that is happening with Wrath, but I definitely need the money. I lean over and whisper to Janet, "So, like, I need to talk to you about publishing stuff. I thought that was why I was here..."

"Your turn is coming up," says Janet, cutting me off.

"What?"

I feel a tap on my shoulder and Shira cries, "Your energy is corrupting the circle. Share your honest desires and then depart! You too, Janet."

Janet nudges me to share, and whispers, "What do you want?"

I take the haunted heart and look into its face. It gives me the creeps.

<hr>

The "class" ends and I walk with Janet out of the court-yard while Shira keeps talking to the women, mentioning some spirit named "Alû" again and again.

We walk in silence to an outdoor tennis court. There are couple of thirty-something men playing. Janet stares at them and remarks, "Tennis erotica and romance, it's an emerging market. My algorithm doesn't know why, but tennis with sex, even with a subpar writer and even a subpar story—it sells very well."

"I never played. I never was much of a sports girl."

Janet nods and continues to watch the game. "Drunks never get into tennis. Only golf, and the occasional skydive. One of my writers, the one you are fucking, played basketball in college. I like working with athletes, they are disciplined and have good habits. Writers, unfortunately, most of them are a fucking disaster, but until robots take your jobs, I am stuck with you."

Jesus, she might even be a bigger cunt than Nora. "Can we talk publishing, not sports or who I am fucking?"

"Wrath has something special, he's not just my token African-American writer; that's why I work with him, same with Shira. But she is special...in her own way."

"Wow. It's not an act?"

Janet shrugs and nods. "I've tried to get her to see someone, but she won't go. She believes psychologists are soul killers. She reminds me of a Scientologist writer I worked with long ago—bad idea, btw, stay away from them. I do feel for Shira. This is how she copes with losing her husband, but you can relate, you turned to writing when you were drying out."

I nod and say, "You sure know an awful lot about me."

"That's my job, sweetie...this business has always involved...less than stable people, but really, there are just two types of writers that can have lasting success in publishing."

My stomach twists and knots. "What are these two types?"

Janet looks away from me again, focusing on a never-ending tennis match. I think it's called a volley: one guy is playing it really aggressively and the other looks like he's just waiting for the perfect shot. "You have a writer like Shira, who is, for lack of better word, nuts. Damaged even. Writing books is the only way she can be whole. And she is so deluded and so passionate, that her book feels so real because of it. It needed no major content editing. It's pure and its mistakes and weaknesses somehow are its strengths. You don't want to tamper with it. You copyedit it and then sell it and thank whoever there is to thank that it came to you."

"So who is the 'other' writer?" I ask, expecting that she'll say me.

She doesn't answer but stares at the tennis player who finally gets that perfect shot and lets out a big *woooh!* cele-bratory yell.

Janet looks back at me and says, "Nora doesn't have genius or that crazy thing Shira has. She's just read a lot of books and has written a lot of books, and thank god she stopped writing literary fiction and chose a genre that people—well, women—actually read. Her books are always beautifully written, but they are also always missing that thing. That thing that Shira's book has, and why it has outsold both of your latests combined.

"So then what am I?"

"Out of a career if you don't do what I am about to ask you."

"And what's that, Janet? You know I have options too. I make money."

"Not like you used to make. Not enough. There are plenty of self-published authors who are doing well, but even they aren't doing as well since Kindle Unlimited. Those writers still making money are also publishing a book every six weeks. Hasn't it been about six months since you published anything?"

"That's not..."

"Be quiet and just listen, Autumn."

"Ok...I'm listening," I huff.

"It's very simple. Get Nora to agree to write a paranormal romance series with you."

I laugh bitterly. "Are you fucking serious. That will never work. I'm sorry, but I am not working with that cu..." I pause trying to remain half-professional. "Bitch."

Janet laughs. "She referred to *you* as a hack cum dumpster diving diva." Like I said, she is good with language."

"She is just a huge bitch."

"So am I, who cares, you'll make money together."

"There has got to be another way."

"If you two could bring your fan bases together, you could make up to seven figures."

"Seven...figures..."

"Seven figures. With a series, hell, maybe eight."

"Well shit," I say, "You should have said that in the first place. I'll pretty much do anything but take a drink for seven figures."

"There's one thing," Nora says, "You are going to have to convince her to work with you, because she won't listen to me when I even try to bring it up, and she's already said no."

CHAPTER FIVE

I hold up the Con itinerary pamphlet and skim the schedule for Nora's name. At 4:00 PM I see Room 07: *Pitch a Hit to Nora Carpenter: You have a character, you have a hook, you have conflict—but do you have a story worth writing? Pitch to Nora and get invaluable feedback that will lead you on the fast track to success.*

I check my phone and see it's 4:53.

My walk no longer has the same I-just-had-great-sex strut as I make it to Room 07.

I peek inside and see so many women with depressed faces who I assume have already queried Nora. The 'pitch line' only has a few women left. I can feel their nerves echoing my own. Some stand with fake confidence. Others are slumping and jittery. We are all scared of Nora.

I never had to go through the pitch, query, or professional editing process. Whatever I created I always felt was good enough. This pitch stuff looks miserable and humiliating. I walk in on Nora chewing out a woman who looks to be on the verge of tears.

I try to hide in the back but the last woman in line

looks at me. She has short blond hair and looks like a depressed bank teller. "Oh wow," she says to me, "What are you doing here? You should be up front there with Nora."

"I guess I am here to...watch and learn. To observe young writers and continue to grow myself."

"Wow, you are so cool and humble!" she says and puts out her hand to introduce herself. "Hey, I am Wilma, and I am a big fan."

"Autumn," I say and shake her hand.

Wilma looks back at Nora who is just about done eviscerating the latest pitch. "She is kind of intimidating."

"Yeah, a little bit."

"Could you um... listen to my pitch and synopsis and give me some feedback?"

I learned the lesson to always say no when women e-mailed me their story ideas. If I gave them bad feedback, many times they'd end up giving me a bad review on Amazon. If I gave them good feedback, they'd keep e-mailing me for more help.

It's a lot easier to just ignore anyone online, but being face to face with Wilma, I don't know how to say no. "Sure. Maybe I can give you give you a pointer or two."

Wilma smiles with gratitude. "Thank you. I still haven't voted yet for tonight's award, but now, I am definitely leaning toward voting for *you*."

I almost forgot about the awards. I know I'm not winning. The fourth woman, who couldn't make it, maybe she has a shot, but everyone knows it is Shira's.

I nod awkwardly. "Ugh, thanks. Well, ok, pitch me."

Her eyes light up and she says, "OK, the name of my book is *The Ghost's Gardener*."

"Interesting title. Um... good alliteration."

"Cool. Thanks so much!"

I'm afraid to ask more. "So...what is it about?"

"Ok, ok, so picture this," she says with wide-eyed excitement. "It's about a good Texas girl who inherits her grandfather's estate. She is twenty two and still a virgin because she believes in real love. When she sleeps at night she sees a scary man in a poncho riding a donkey. She learns that a bunch of Mexican ghosts are haunting her estate, but it gets better, there is a man who once stopped the Mexican uprising. A good-looking man, with an even better heart. But my heroine, she is no damsel in distress... she knows how to use a pistol and even brown ghosts can bleed. Through bloodshed and redemption she will heal wounds and know true love...What do you think?"

Sadly, racist paranormal romance actually does pretty well. "That's something else...wow...you know, I am not qualified to really give feedback, but I bet Nora will have something to say...looks like you're next."

I watch Nora's facial expression go from annoyed to outraged within few seconds of Wilma's *The Ghost's Gardener* pitch. When Wilma finishes, Nora laughs hysterically and exclaims, "Why?! Why even write something like that?"

"Excuse me."

"This is an atrocious book idea. Listen to me, this is tough love. Go do anything else with your life. Don't write fiction and get woke or whatever the millennials call it."

"Gosh, you don't have to be rude!" The woman, getting teary-eyed says, "I just want to express myself."

"Then go write some shitty Instagram poetry," Nora slams back.

"Bu...bu...but..." Wilma stutters, but can only say, "Bitch," and crumbles her pitch paper, throwing it at Nora.

It bounces off her head and Nora's mouth drops in shock. "What are you, twelve?!"

Wilma storms out of the room, leaving just the two of us. Nora shakes her head and says to me, "What do you want, Autumn?"

I force myself to take a deep breath. "Look, Nora. I just wanted to clear the air. You know earlier... I feel like we got off on the wrong foot."

"No, we didn't."

"Um...what?"

"I know you talked to my agent, I saw you two canoodling by the tennis court."

"She thought we could really compliment each other." I feel myself sinking into the floor, my self esteem, a bug being squashed beneath her heels.

"Stop right there. I'm too tired to be tactful, so let me just say it. You are just a shitty writer, Autumn. Your face should be on the first page of a Wikipedia article on hacks. You just got lucky that being in rehab helped you produce a few plot-driven yarn spinners."

"Look, I don't like your boring ass books either. But I need an advance, and I'm not blessed in life like you. I don't have an MFA, and connections...basically Janet says we can split seven figures if we work together. Look, I don't want to work with you either."

"Is that so, Autumn? I feel so honored," Nora says and rolls her eyes."

"I didn't mean it like that...it's just that we can make good money together."

"You know what, Autumn, I have a lot of literary fiction writer 'friends', people who I got an MFA with years ago, and they assume what I do is purely for money. They think because I'm not writing about malaise and ennui in the suburbs, I am just some artistic prostitute. But I care about the craft and followed my muse to this genre and have single handedly raised it up. I'm comfortable and proud of it, and if I work with you then my MFA friends are right about me."

"You have been shitty and cunty to me from the get go, you have thrown shade at me since my first book broke out."

"Ugh, don't toss your idiotic millennial aphorisms at me."

"Jesus Christ, Nora...you sound like my mo..." I stop there, knowing that could be too low of a blow.

"Listen, I'm the most successful writer in this genre, and did you ever try to listen to my criticism or reach out to me for help? Nope. Did you try to give back to others? Nope. Did you message or e-mail me or anyone for guidance? Nope. Instead you acted like hot shit who believed she had discovered the secret to storytelling after her first book. The natural. But now your lack of craft is showing, and you're stuck. Tough titties, cause I've worked my ass off to get here and I write in this specific genre because I love it. I'm just as serious as Franzen or whatever over-rated white man Oprah is having a parade for this year. I care about the craft of fiction, but I don't think you do or ever will."

"I do care. Finding out I could tell stories saved me. I really do care, but I also need to pay my bills, and I...I have writer's block."

"You care more about the money and being loved than the craft itself—just like my agent—but that is why she sells books instead of writes them. You have never once asked for genuine help and now are just trying to use me to save your ass. I'm not into it."

I want to tell her that is total bullshit, but it's kind of true. Writing being hard all of sudden has taken away what I loved about it in the first place. I want to get better, I just don't know how. I need to get paid and figure out what to do next...but this stupid petty bitch doesn't want to help me, she just wants to shit on me. Fuck her. "Be honest, Nora, you just don't like me. That is what this is about. You're just really fucking jealous of me, and seeing me fail is more important to you than making half-a-million dollars. Women like you are all alike."

Nora condescendingly laughs. "Women like me?"

"Yes, women like you, who enjoy seeing women like me grovel and suffer. From my mother, to my teachers, to you, you've all treated me the same. Well, fuck this, I rather cam on Chaturbate than work with you. So congrats, you have less competition now, go and celebrate. You and Shira can battle it out for the Queen of Paranormal Romance."

"Shira might be a nutbag but at least she cares about craft."

"Then go work with her. I'm so over this. I'm leaving this stupid ass Con. I knew it would be a waste of time."

CHAPTER SIX

I GO BACK TO MY ROOM AND START PACKING UP MY suitcase. Going to this Con was such a stupid idea. At least I got laid and sold some books. I think about texting Wrath, but I kinda wanna just keep this a drama free fling.

Weirdly, it didn't feel like a fling, but anyway, he lives in Texas. A long distance relationship is the last thing I need right now. I need to go back, start up a pot of coffee and put all this fucking frustration into the best book I'll ever write—I can find my magic again.

I close my suitcase and walk out of the room. The sound of tears and moaning meets me at the end of the hallway. I spot a figure crouching against the wall by the exit. I roll down a few more feet and realize it's Shira.

I try to imagine myself just walking past her but when I see her, I can't. She is grasping the Haunted Heart Award, staring into its creepy eyes.

"I feel ya, Shira," I say. "This event is one big shit show."

She wipes the mascara and tears from her cheeks and glances sideways at my suitcase. "You're leaving?"

"I think so. I think it is time for me to go."

Shira nods. "I wish I could leave too. But the spirits and my husband said I have to be at the award ceremony. They say I can't go home again, they say that the hotel will be my new home."

She gives me flashbacks of some of the girls I met in rehab. The ones that did too much meth and believed crazy shit, but Shira isn't a meth head, she's just still temporarily insane from grief. "Shira, my heart really goes out to you..."

"I miss him so much. I can hear his voice when the spirits talk to me...but he sounds so different now. Death has changed him. I want him back so bad. It's not fair! He should be here with me..."

Shira slams her fist against the wall as more tears flow down her face.

God damn it...now I'm starting tear up too...

I lean my suitcase against the wall and hug Shira.

Her tears drip down my bare shoulders. They give me a chill. I can feel her hurt and loss, and a deep gaping loneliness that frightens me.

"The worst is the spirits have been really mean to me lately. They only seem to care about the award ceremony now. I feel so lonely. So lost."

I hold her closer to me. "I think the award ceremony is going to be good for you. You are going to win the damn thing, and I think winning it and honoring him is going to help you move on. I really do."

"They said I would find peace in winning the award, and that it would unleash my true love."

"I think your husband...or maybe you, are looking to let go tonight."

"Maybe."

"I believe so," I say, extending my hand to her. "Come on, let's go back to your room and get you ready for tonight. You should fix yourself up so you look nice when you win the award."

Shira holds onto the award and says, "Ok, but first I have to drop this off to the Con people. I'll be ok. I can get ready myself."

"You sure?"

"Yeah, and you're right, I will win, and then I gotta... probably move on. Maybe write another book or something."

"I can relate to that. You'll be ok."

"Thanks, Autumn."

"No problem, Shira"

"Sorry for calling you a poser."

"It's ok, you were sort of right."

She nods, "Well, sorry to see you go. Have a safe ride home."

"Thanks," I say, thinking of Wrath. "Actually, I think I'm going to stay."

I feel nervous, knocking on Wrath's door.

The door swings open. "Hey beautiful ..." he says, but his smile vanishes when he looks down at my suitcase. "What's up? You're not leaving, are you? I thought you were gonna be my date tonight."

I sigh and say, "Can we talk?"

"Yeah," he says, "I was about to text you to come up."

I follow him inside and put my suitcase against the wall. "I was going to leave, but talking to Shira..."

"Shira? Why? Did you get my texts? I wanted to know how it went with Nora...I guess it didn't go so well."

"No, it didn't," I say, with a sigh.

"Talk to me," he says, his hand caressing my back. "What happened."

"I liked writing because I didn't really have to deal with people, but now I have to deal with all kinds of bullshit and ass kiss these petty bitches. I was ready to leave, but Shira, out of all people gave me second thoughts...in a weird way, she showed me that there's something here with us, something special..."

Wrath puts his fingers on my lips and kisses me.

His embrace feels more like home than the empty bed I have waiting for me in Ashland.

He gazes into my eyes. "So what the hell happened?"

"I got an ultimatum from Janet to do a series with Nora. I didn't want to, but it could be for seven figures. So I went and asked Nora, but of course she acted super cunty and told me I was a shit writer."

Wrath nods thoughtfully and says, "You know, my ex hated talking anything writing related. She said it just made me stressed, and I'd be better off teaching high school English and that Austin needs teachers, and I'm just being selfish. But I kept getting work, and I am addicted to that feeling of getting lost in a story and living the life of my characters."

I smile, remembering transcribing my first book and uploading it to reach readers. "I miss that feeling. It's just not working for me anymore. I keep sputtering out."

"I was lucky. Guys like Brian Keene and Ed Lee took me under their wing and taught me the craft. Then I met some romance writers like Tiffany Reisz and even Nora. I humbled myself and now, I don't get writer's block. Janet knows what she is doing."

"Nora refuses to work with me and she rubbed it in my face. Even if Nora agreed to work with me, how would I do it without murdering her...I wish I could work with you, or hell, any man instead. Men aren't cunts...maybe she's right, maybe I'm not a real writer. Maybe, I really did just get lucky."

"Nah," he said. "You only got lucky meeting me."

"I'm serious," I say and slap him little too hard, part me of angry that he's trying to keep me from being pissed off.

"I am serious too. You're a real writer, you just have to humble your ass and respect the craft. And I got your back. Alright? We'll figure this out. There is a way, there's always a way. Writers are like video games, they all have cheat codes."

———

Wrath fixes his bowtie but keeps sneaking looks at me tightening my dress in front of the mirror. "Damn, you look fine."

"At least I'll look good going to my career's funeral."

Wrath laughs and says, "Come on."

I nod, but I feel like no matter how I approach her now, she is going to reject me.

Wrath is a nice distraction. "I find some consolation that at least I'll be with the hottest guy in the room."

Wrath playfully mock pops his collar and walks toward me.

He holds me close and gazes at me in the reflection. I can't ever recall meeting a guy who made me feel so safe and so turned on at the same time. I just want stay in bed and order room service for the rest of the weekend.

He extends the crook of his arm. "Let's go to the ball."

I slip my arm through his and we walk out of the room toward the elevator. We kiss until we hear the doorbell.

It feels so good to walk to the ballroom. I see my books displayed in the book nook near the desserts. Then I spot Nora at the bar. She is wearing a gold dress and the same old stink eye glaring in our direction.

Her smug face slowly morphs into a smile as she looks

at Wrath, pretending I'm not even there. "Good to see you, Wrath. Slumming it after your divorce?"

Wrath's face turns stony and I feel mine going red. "Ugh...hey Nora."

"Hello dear," Nora says with side-eye. "The nominees, I've just learned have to sit together....Mr. Wrath why don't you lead us to our table, so we can have some girl talk."

He moves ahead of us looking annoyed. Nora grabs her drink. I stare at his tight butt in his black dress pants like it will provide me with the needed strength, but it does not. Nora is staring at it too and says, "Agh...to be young again," she sighs. "I miss having Con flings. Enjoy him for now, he'll probably remarry an organic soap girl or a bass player in six months."

"Are you naturally a cunt, or is it just like your literary persona?"

"Both."

Janet is sitting with PhD. God damn it, they have us sitting together. I glance at the vodka and cranberry Janet is stirring. The way the light hits the glass it looks like she is drinking delicious blood.

Janet looks up and says, "Nora. Autumn. I made sure you two could sit next to each other."

Nora scowls and says, "Nope. I'm not doing this, Janet. I'd rather teach hacks having a mid-life crisis at a low-residency MFA program than work with her. No way."

Janet sighs and PhD says, "from a scholarly point of view, you two working together could really add a new and exciting layer to a genre that I love but still remains quite unambitious, historically speaking of course."

"Jesus Christ, Alexandra, you're an overpaid librarian, nothing more nothing less, please leave my writing career out of your thesis," Nora says.

Janet slams her bloody looking drink on the table. "Will you twats stop acting like a bunch of high school mean girl cheerleaders and be cordial!"

Nora sits down and says, "I'd rather work with Shira, at least *she* can write."

"You will have a new agent if you don't sit down here, and at least try to get along for this dinner."

I don't even know what to say. Wrath squeezes my hand under the table.

CHAPTER SEVEN

The awkward silence and polite claps continue as the awards are given out. Every time I even attempt to talk to Nora she just ignores me. Each minute that passes by, I hate her more, until finally, I ignore her too.

Wrath grips my sweaty hand.

I wish Shira would come sit with us, strangely, she might make this less awkward. But she is sitting at the bar looking like she's in deep meditation or mid séance—god only knows.

I watch Fabio give awards to women I used to outsell. I should just quit. There have to be other jobs out there for me. Something less soul-draining.

Fabio continues to smile moronically at the crowd. "Okay everybody, I having such great time. Next up we have best paranormal romance debut."

The claps start again and I can remember when I was nominated but didn't win. I didn't care because I was getting paid, but now, it would actually feel good to win something. Something to get my confidence going again.

I let go of Wrath's hand and whisper in his ear, "Can you get some air with me, for a min?"

He nods and grabs my hand, leading me out of the ballroom to the stairs and elevator. I see us in the mirror and he says, "We really do make a good couple."

I smile and say, "We do," and wonder what the hell is going to happen when we both have to go home tomorrow.

He nods and laughs. "Damn, I haven't been to a dinner that awkward since my ex told her folks we were getting divorced."

"I know. I see now it's just not going to happen with Nora, and honestly I don't even want to work with her. I don't need a big press or agent; I just need someone to help. And I fucking hate working with women, I can't do it, not even if my damn life depends on it and it sort of does."

"You can't give up. Go apologize to her and find a way to make it work with Nora. Janet is right. You guys working together would help you grow."

I feel a little betrayed, but I look at him and picture us writing something together, being inspired by our chemistry. "What if I work with you? What if we wrote something together? You've got the experience, I'm good at coming up with hooks. If our writing chemistry is half as good as our actual chemistry, we can self-publish some hits together."

Wrath pauses and for the first time since we've met he looks annoyed with me. "What? No, that is a bad idea. No way."

"Why? What, you can only fuck women writers, but you can't work with them?"

"I didn't say that. Look, I don't cum where I work and our styles just wouldn't mesh. Your style would actually complement Nora's and vice versa, but not mine."

"You just don't want to talk to me after the Con," I say, losing my cool. "You're looking for an out."

"What the fuck?! Are you serious?"

"I am. I guess you are not."

"Aw hell no. I don't need this."

"What the fuck, Wrath. Really? You know, I could use some support."

"Well, I could use a cigar right now."

"A cigar? Now?"

"I am going to the roof and I am smoking a cigar. I am not one for drama and you're just starting a shitload of it right now."

"Oh fuck you, you just don't want to have a real conversation about what we are going to do when the Con is over."

"You keep telling yourself that, and you keep telling yourself that you don't need help and you know better than everyone else."

"You are just intimidated to work with a woman who sells more books than you."

"Yeah, that's it. I'm going to go smoke my cigar. Good luck with the award show," he says, storming off.

"Whatever, go have your fucking cigar."

I walk back to the award ceremony and keep glancing over at the bar. I feel so alone, especially when I return to my seat next to Nora.

"Don't feel bad, honey," Nora whispers to me. "He's more faithful to his cigars than his side bitches. That's the term for you, right, side bitch? I seriously can't keep up with these millennial terms."

I grit my teeth and glance at Janet, drinking her fourth vodka and cranberry. I get why the program says, you need a higher power, because I need a miracle right now to stop me from getting a drink. I know my health is fucked, but what if I could stop at two, maybe two and ½ drinks?

Fuck...this is bad. Damn this bad...I stare back at the bar and notice that the bartender is also a dealer, when I notice her giving a white packet of something to one of the waiters. Pills would be nice right about now.

Fabio goes back onstage and I signal the waitress who has been serving the table.

She comes over and asks, "What can I get for you?"

"Vodka, on the rocks. Please make sure it is here after this award is called out."

"Um, ok. Are you sure?" she says, giving me a look of concern.

Damn it, she's a fan. "Um...I'm not sure-sure. Shit... just come back to me after the award. Ok."

She nods and goes to another table.

I know that drinking won't help. I know this logically, I really do. It's passive aggressive, self-destructive, and a cry for help. I can hear my counselor's voice in my head telling me this, but that feeling in my stomach—I hate it, and drinking has been the only thing that makes it go away.

I look away from these bitches enjoying their drinks and back towards the stage. Fabio approaches the microphone, beaming at the crowd. I've never found him attractive but I get it; he just looks so happy all the time. There's a weird sense of hope Fabio radiates. I wish I had a fraction of that.

He adjusts the microphone to reach his height and leans his arm on the podium. "I'm having such good time, it make me sad that ceremony is about to end. Our next award is one I can relate to cause I'm so old I am getting close to death, ah-ha-ha-ha. But I still have great hair," the crowd laughs harder than it should. "The presenter for the award for Best Paranormal Romance Novel of the year will be last year winner's Samantha Guillotine. Aw, she's so beautiful."

Samantha does the whitest white girl happy dance I've ever seen as she goes up to the stage. She gives Fabio a huge hug. Her feet fly up in the air as he swings her up. Putting her back down, he bows to her with absurd flourish, before strutting off the stage.

Samantha smiles and waves at the crowd. "Hey everybody, this is so exciting! The big moment has finally arrived. I am just ecstatic to give out The Haunted Heart Award tonight. I know Shira had it blessed, so it is somehow even more of a super special award now."

Everyone laughs, except Shira, who has her head down at the bar, looking like she is either praying or cursing.

Samantha calls out the nominees and I hear Shira mumbling to herself behind the curtain of her long dark hair. "Our love and your restless soul will be consummated with this award. It will free you and our love will have a tangible outlet, and we will finally feel true bliss and peace...." Shira chants, "Alû abada dey bey dend abo Alû."

Shira's prayer chant ends when Samantha says, "And the winner for best paranormal romance novel is...oh, it was my favorite too. *Immortally Yours* by Angie Foxx."

Almost everyone's mouth drops including mine.

Holy shit, the three of us must have split the award, that D-Lister mousey bitch Angie Foxx got it.

Once the shock subsides, loud claps flood the dinning hall as a smiling Foxx walks to the stage to receive the award, but Shira is following right behind her onto the stage.

Shira swipes the award from Samantha and holds it up.

PhD shakes her head and says, "Oh my god, she's pulling a Paranormanye."

"What's the hell does that mean?" asks Janet.

"Like what Kanye did to Taylor Swift but with Paranormal Romance."

The whole thing is so absurd that I laugh. This whole Con really is a fucking disaster.

Shira holds up the award like she is Moses showing off the commandments. The golden heart reflects the shocked faces in the crowd. Shira glares at them, seething with rage and says, "Look at all of you, thinking you know love and the spirits; writing and reading books that lack art and humanity, just preying on the fears and desires of the lonely. You have no sense of what art is and no sense of the truth. I am living a real paranormal romance! You think writing about spirits and love has no consequences. You think this is just all fun and games. It's not! My husband is a real ghost and my real love is here and he is angry and so are his friends. Making money off their suffering, telling stories for fun. Those are the true horrors. And even worse, not rewarding my story. My truth! My art! You not only rejected me, you rejected honoring the spirits. Now you can answer to them."

I roll my eyes and laugh but then see the heart start beating; the lights dim, the tables shake, and the dining room doors slam shut.

CHAPTER EIGHT

Shira looks down in shock at the heart in her hands that is beating faster and faster until it finally bursts open.

A loud pop echoes through the ballroom and an angry ghoulish specter flies out of the broken award. It has white translucent skin and a bald head. Its demonic eyes glow deep red.

It's the same face that was on the award.

The award is repairing itself, becoming whole again...

What...the...fuck...

Shira gazes aghast into the spirit's eyes. "You... you... you're not my husband, you're..."

"Holy fuck!" I scream, as the spirit expands and floats upwards.

It looks away from Shira and smiles at me. It scans the room, focusing on the male waiters and husbands of all the frightened paranormal romance fans and writers.

"These men's hearts, are not pure, not worthy human men at all, but they shall give me power," the demonic spirit bellows.

The specter points its long grimey fingers at the men

and makes a 'come hither' gesture with its index finger. Every single man in the place floats helplessly up into the air, their faces cringe and get as red as the specter's eyes.

It smiles and says, "I hate the sound of the hearts of men. Like dim witted clocks." Their chests explode, ribs flying, and their still beating hearts soar into the demon's body. Its flesh absorbs all their hearts, like they are souls being sucked into a new hell. Each heart adds definition to its body, filling out its flesh.

It shifts its attention to me and the others at the nominees' table. "Ah yes, that's better, but my dears, you are the souls I want. The worthy ones. For I am Alû and I will…"

A crying male voice interrupts the demonic spirit, "Oh no, oh dear God, no. …Save me, please Lord Jesus, Middle East God, Jew God, whoever calls the shots. Help me please…"

I realize it's Fabio crying in the corner of the sage. The demon smiles at a scared to death Fabio and floats up to him. "I like your hair, mine was burned off many years ago."

Alû grabs a long strand of Fabio's hair. The hair absorbs into the specter's finger, turning black on contact. More and more hair gets eaten into the spirit, until Fabio is bald and Alû has long dark hair flowing down to his shoulders.

Fabio's skin dries and prunes, but he's alive. Alû looks down at him, rips the skin off his own wrist and shoves it into a choking Fabio's mouth.

"My flesh, my truth, you shall be it, to ward off those who are not worthy to play with me."

"No, you lied!" Shira screams, as tears flow down her face. "You are not my beloved. You never were."

Alû turns to her. "Your husband was a good man, so his soul is not mine, but your heartache called me and touched my own dark heart. Oh my dear Shira, you have helped me escape my prison and brought me to a buffet of beatitudes of dark romance." He licks his lips and stares at me and the others. "You have freed me and brought me to where my fate has wanted to go since man drew his first breath."

"No," Shira screams. She looks at me and the others. "I'm so sorry. I didn't know...I'm so sorry. He's for me, just me..."

Alû looks at her with a disturbing blend of sadism and pity. "Dear Shira, don't flatter yourself. I already have your soul. I just needed you to get me here," he looks back out into the crowd. "So many women. So many dreams and heartaches. So much fun to be had. Who will be the one? I already know, but do you? You, dear Shira, are not the one. You never were. Now come to me. Let me finally digest your soul."

Alû beckons Shira and lifts her into the air. Shira kicks and fights but he has full control of her body. The blackened heart trophy lying on the podium begins to beat again. The heartbeat thumps faster and louder the closer Shira gets.

"Help me," Shira cries out to us.

But we can't.

Aghast, we watch Alû pick up the haunted heart award. The heart beat stops and its mouth opens. Shira screams as the mouth sucks her up like a vacuum. I expect blood and the shredding of flesh, but the heart swallows her whole—absorbing her entire essence.

Then the heart beats again, louder.

Alû caresses the heart trophy and stares at us. "Months and months of hearing about her mundane heartache. Ugh, what boredom. You women have evolved so much, but my favorites were the Neanderthals. Such simple but effective storytellers. Their caves always called to me. But now, I have found true romancers worthy of me."

He turns his eyes away from us and directs his attention towards the book nook. His eyes turn red, the books open, and all the pages start flipping on their own. His eyes turn black; it almost looks like he's reading the pages.

"Yes, yes, yes, this shall be glorious," he says, as all the books fly off the table and are sucked through the heart's face mouth. The heart stays the same size but the beat speeds up.

Alû looks back at us. The heart and him seem to be intertwined. The heartbeat grows louder as it grows behind him, "I haven't been free since the Sanctus Bello Regalem. Let us begin, my beauties."

Alû spreads out his batlike black wings. I duck down as he soars past me, feeling his heat and rage as a tangible dark electricity in the air. Women scream and cry as Alû flies around, taunting and laughing at them.

I keep waiting for him to attack any of the other women here, but he seems to be enjoying inflicting fear more than pain.

He stares back at the Haunted Heart Award and says, "Build my house, use the women as wood."

Alû flies out through the dining hall doors and I am ready to breathe a sigh of relief, but then the blackened heart award stops beating and explodes like bomb, the black guts or whatever it is inside of it land on the wall still connected to the Haunted Heart Sandard. The white flower wallpaper gets splats of the black guts, but the black doesn't dry, it moves like the guts are hungry veins, crawling all over the walls, like a spiderweb covering every inch to make a home.

Shit, this whole floor is going to be swallowed up in gooey blackness.

I look at Nora and the other women. "We need to get the fuck out of here. Run! Now!"

For the first time ever, we run together. We run as fast as we can to the hotel exit, but the black veins are spreading fast, faster than we can run to reach the lobby.

We look toward the exit doors but they are covered in black goo and pulsing bloody veins.

"Open it!" Nora orders.

"I don't think we should touch it," PhD says.

"Kick it open!" screams Nora.

"Fuck that, I'm not touching it!" I reply.

I hear clunky heels and see Wilma running up. She pushes us out of the way to get near the door. "I have to get out, I have to get out. Now!" She attempts to kick it open, but her foot gets stuck in the black goo, never even hitting the glass. The black veins wrap themselves around her legs and pull her into the bloody veined black door.

She hangs upside down, her arms extending as far as they can to us. "Help me!" she screams.

I try to reach out to her but she keeps sinking into the black goo. The black goo pulls her away and she is sucked down like a water slide into nothingness.

Gone. No trace of her except the echo of her scream.

I stare into the black veined walls, the heartbeat vibrates through veins, with each body, or even soul, it gets louder and stronger.

"We need to tell the other women," I say. "We need to warn them to not touch the blackness."

Janet shakes her head says, "If they're dumb enough to touch it, then fuck them. We need to figure out a way out of this...ladies, we need to try to make a deal with this demon. It's the best course of action."

"Jesus, Janet," Nora exclaims.

" Just hear me out..." Janet says, with a surprising lack of panic. "Maybe we can give him a certain amount of girls and leave?"

"This isn't a fucking book deal," Nora rages back. "He's a god damn demon that wants a buffet of paranormal romance fans and writers, not some hack horror writer..."

A choir of screams echo out of the lobby, and it makes my bones go cold.

I look back down the lobby and see a throng of frightened women running toward us. I turn around at the stairs to the second floor, and there are no black veins on it.

"Let's run up the stairs!" I scream. " We gotta run *now*."

Nora shakes her head and shoots back. "Are you fucking suicidal? No, we need to find a way out! Let's check the back way, the emergency exit."

I want to run up those stairs. Everything inside me tells me that is the best way we can survive, but I worry that being alone could be a death sentence in itself. God damn it...I hope Nora's right, as I run with her and the other women to the emergency exit.

We go in the opposite direction of all the screaming women and head to the first floor emergency exit. The black veins have spread over everything except the glass door of the emergency exit.

Something doesn't seem right about it. I pause and catch my breath, and out of habit reach for my phone. I remember that Wrath is up there, and hopefully safe. I try to call the police but there's no reception. I try to text Wrath to call for help, but nothing goes through.

I put my phone back in my purse and stare at the emergency exit.

"Maybe it can't go on the glass?" Janet asks.

I stare into it and don't see an exit. It's formless. I'm not a fucking scientist but this doesn't seem to align with the basic laws I know of physics. And my gut screams to not open it.

Janet takes her house keys out of her purse and throws them at the door. The key knocks off the door and little cracks spread through the glass door.

Nora breathes with relief.

But the glass keeps cracking.

I scream, "Get back!"

The glass explodes and shatters. A hand reaches out of the mist, trying to grab Nora.

The hand is rugged and strong. Dirty and human.

The scariest part is I recognize the hand. Nora backs away and a PhD and Janet stare in disbelief, and then it hits me. I know who that hand belongs to.

This is bad. Really bad.

CHAPTER NINE

OH MY GOD, THIS CAN'T BE POSSIBLE...I STARE AT THE 18th century man...he's...no this can't be...

Janet grabs a fire extinguishers from the wall, as I stare at a man that I have never *seen,* but know almost intimately—Colonel John Riverson— the charming and troubled love interest from my historical romance novel *The Ghost of Galveston.*

As my face goes white, I wonder if this is a dream or if we've somehow been drugged.

The Colonel stretches his 6'4 frame and smiles at me. "Aw my dear Autumn. You recognize me! I've waited so long to be real. Bless Alû, through him all is possible."

"What the fuck," I say. "Do you see what I see?"

"I see John Riverson, the protagonist from your third novel," PhD exclaims. "He's...exactly how I pictured him..."

"Oh yes, it is I, madam," he says, his lips stretching into a toothy grin full of demonic jagged teeth that could shred anything in one bite. "Join me, join Alû in his heaven, in his heart, my beloveds. All of you. Come to me now and let me taste you through him."

"Fuck! Fuck! Fuck! This is fucking real!" I scream. "What the fuck?!?!?"

"So very real," he says, as long talons spring out of his hands. "But please, watch your mouths. Ladies do not speak such filth. You must be disciplined."

He leaps forward with talons out, swiping at Nora, missing her only by a few inches.

I try to run away, but on my third step, my right heel trips over PhD's. I fall to the ground but Riverson turns his attention from Nora to Janet. "You aren't worthy of being here, I'll shall dispose of you."

He growls and licks his lips, ready to lunge, but Janet takes the fire extinguisher from the wall and slams it against his skull.

Black goo drips out of his mouth, over jagged teeth and onto the floor. Janet pounds his skull again and again, but he laughs, his head still intact. "Foolish trollop. Ghosts and spirits cannot die."

Janet tries to strike him again, but the extinguisher slips out her hands and rolls to my feet.

The colonel uses his talons to lift himself from the carpeted floor and stands up, grinning with his jagged teeth. I stare down at the extinguisher and remember his human death was from freezing in the harsh winters of Maine. Could he have a weakness? Is the point of this to figure out how to beat my own creations?

I shoot half of the cold foam from the fire extinguisher into his face and hold it up as a shield, anticipating his lunge, but the colonel looks at me with sadness.

His face melts along with his body and merges back into black gooed veins that slither in the walls.

We catch our breath but the screams only get closer, louder. "We need to go upstairs, ok," I tell the other women, holding onto the fire extinguisher. "We should have done that in the first place.

Nora tries her best to compose herself but shakes her head. "We don't know what the hell is out there. For fuck sakes, there are fictional characters coming out of goddamn windows!"

"We will figure it out on the next floor," I bark back.

"I might have a theory, as to what is happening," PhD says.

More screams of the women echo through the halls and I say, "Tell me on the next floor, we need to go—now!"

Adrenaline and survival instincts drive me forward. We run back into the lobby, our heels clicking and echoing like experimental drum beats mixing in with all the horrifying screams.

We make it to the stairs, but then I see why the women are screaming. Fabio is standing in front of the stairs holding three horrified and struggling women. The skin of his face is gone and flesh keeps dripping off his revived corpse. His demonic red eyes look down at his captors. His muscles are twice the size as when he was alive; he has hair everywhere except for his head, he looks more like a bigfoot monster from...

Holy shit...the bigfoot monster the Colonel John Riverson fights in the *The Ghost of Galveston* book.

What...the...fuck...why is my book coming alive?

Bigfoot Fabio takes all three women and heaves them into the throbbing black veined hotel walls.

"Not Fabio, why did it have to turn Fabio. That's just evil!" Nora cries out.

Fabio heaves another girl in the black wall and then stares at us.

"Ay yeah," Bigfoot Fabio says, "Look at all these pretty

pretty ladies of appropriate age." He shows a crooked grin, his teeth are rotting and fanged just like the Colonel's. "Alû make me feel young again. Give me hair all over, instead of head. The more souls I give him, the younger I am. Come, pretty ladies. I make it quick."

"Do the fire extinguisher thing again. Spray him!" Nora yells.

"Maybe it's like Ghostbusters," Janet says. "Spray him!"

I have a little left and I shoot it right at Fabio's face. The white foam lands on his head and drips off his bald head. He grins and wipes the foam off his face, licking it off his hands. "Ha, I can't believe I'll never die. Get the joke. Funny, right?"

I throw the fire extinguisher at him but he swipes it away and it ricochets, hitting a running fangirl, knocking her into the throbbing black goo veins of the haunted hotel walls.

Bigfoot Fabio stares at Janet, a serpent tongue comes out of his mouth and he licks his lip. "Oh, dear Janet. I still remember your rejection for my novel. You remember that? When I submitted to you and you said I was a no talent hack? I wanted to be taken seriously as a writer instead of just being on covers as a pretty boy, but now, you will know serious pain...see, that good line. Bet you wish you published my book now!"

"Run up the stairs, go now!" I yell.

Fabio runs toward her, while the others try to run up the stairs.

"You cunts," Janet says without emotion and reaches into her pocketbook.

"Run, Janet!" Nora screams.

But Janet stands still and takes out a 100-calorie bag of Blue Diamond Almonds. She rips the bag open and throws them at Fabio's face. A few land in his rotten mouth and one gets lodged into his sunken red eyes.

I cringe from the staircase expecting Janet to be either devoured or tortured by beastly Fabio, but instead acidic black foam drips out of his mouth.

Fabio's hairy body falls to the ground and convulses, puking out, "Help me."

"Nuts," Janet says, watching Fabio's body shrivel and dissipate. "I remember in your book, Autumn, that the sasquatch ghost was deathly allergic to nuts. It was how your protagonist stopped him."

Shit, she's right.

But I still don't know why the hell my fictional world is entering this one, and I don't have time to answer it—the black veins from the walls are spreading, they are going to cover the whole first floor.

"Run up now, Janet," I scream at her.

Janet quickly turns around and sees the veins spreading like a predatory blob looking for food. It absorbs a woman who had been hiding behind a couch and slithers toward Fabio's decaying flesh.

"Fuck me!" Janet says and runs to us on the second floor.

The black veins spread fast until they cover the entire first floor, but it doesn't go up the steps to us.

We are safe, for now.

CHAPTER TEN

THERE ARE NO MORE STAIRS. WE EITHER HAVE TO take the elevator or the fire escape to get to the top. I look back down at the steps. They are covered with black veins. All we can do is keep going and find a way out through the second floor.

"Ok, ok, ok," I say. "But before we go anywhere, we need to figure out what the hell is happening."

"I don't know, Autumn," Nora says and rolls her eyes. "Maybe, we should FaceTime the demon and get the real scoop; anybody got a fucking Ouija Board hanging around. We could try *that*."

I sigh, and PhD says, "Ouija Boards don't really work."

"Jesus, it's like the tower of Babble with the three of you. Solutions. Speak them. Now!" I exclaim.

"Babble...Babylon, yes," PhD nods solemnly to herself. "I think I might have a theory."

"Oh Jesus," Nora says, "We are so fucked."

"Shut up," Janet screams, "All of you shut up, you are going to leave high school behind and realize we are in

Hell if we don't figure out this out. Speak now, Alexandra!"

Nora nods in agreement. "Alright, PhD, do you know who the fuck this Alû thing is?"

"I think I can remember a footnote," she says with uncertainty. "I used it to pad up my thesis and give a fun little anecdote. It was forgettable."

"Today, PhD," Nora orders.

"I remember reading about a warning tale for women who started to tell stories of romance and spirits in ancient Babylon. Women who were widowed or without love started to tell stories to feel less alone, and then they acted out in very strange ways."

"So a boogey man for bored unsatisfied Babylonian women?" I ask.

"Sort of," PhD answers me. "he would seduce women through otherworldly spirits, and then take their souls— a spirit that thrives on female pain."

"So we are facing demonic Christian Grey??" Nora exclaims.

"Um...I don't know," PhD says, "I am trying to remember what I rea..."

A sound comes out of my purse that makes us jump and scream, but we calm down when we realize it's the song, Pony, by Ginuwine—my ringtone for Wrath.

"It's my phone, it's working now," I say. "It's Wrath's.... oh shit, Wrath! Please be ok..."

I reach inside in my purse, and see its FaceTime.

I answer and the phone shows a sky filled with dark clouds. I see the bright blue Marriott letters. Shit, Wrath is still on the roof. At least he is safe.

I let out a sigh of relief but the camera floats up and turns around.

It does a crane shot peering down to a frightened and trembling Wrath. He's lying on his back being held down by a talloned claw. The camera on the phone pans out and we see Alû smiling.

Alû pushes down harder on Wrath's chest and he begs, "Help ... me."

"Silence, *moor*," Alû orders. "Or I will crush you."

Alû brings the phone closer and sniffs it with his flaring nostrils. "Ah, even though these electric currents, I can smell the delicacies that you are, my ladies. Since your cave days I have craved to play with you. Dear Shira has brought me the best of the best. Surrender to me, and you can be my priestesses. We can revel in love and lust and live in delicious torment. Give yourself to my heart, or become part of my gospel."

I stare into those evil eyes. I see a story inside them, a desire, and a flaw that I will have to find to beat him, or he will beat me.

"No," I say, and then look at Wrath. "I'm sorry. I'm so sorry, Wrath."

Alû lets his foot off Wrath's throat and smiles as lightning strikes the hotel. "Very well. Let's have... I believe you call it... *fun*. This hotel is my book, and the floors are its chapters. I hope you enjoy the next one..."

CHAPTER ELEVEN

It's like the lightning has put a spell on the hotel, because the floor has totally changed but yet is so familiar. Instead of the second floor that was there moments ago, it is New Orleans, the setting of my fourth novel. It's exactly how I pictured it even though I've never actually been to New Orleans.

My heroine, Madam Noire told fortunes and fought off spirits while making love with vampires and other dark beasts of the Bayou. I remember a reviewer saying, this book is just a whoreish knock off *True Blood*.

While I try to grasp that the laws of physics no longer exist in the hotel the way they used to, Nora shakes her head in disbelief. "My parents were right, they said pursuing a career writing fiction would ruin my life. I should have quit writing and publishing and gone into advertising."

"So you notice the change too?" PhD asks, staring in disbelief. "Of course you do, cause this is all real now. It's your book again, Autumn."

"I know." I reply.

Janet squints ahead. "I think we should make that

deal, and we make it now. I'd rather be a priestess than a slave. And this place looks very dirty and something tells me it will only get much worse.

Nora looks contemplative. "Better to reign in Hell than be tortured in it. That is logical...but, Autumn is right. You don't make deals with demons, assholes and sadists, and this Alû is all three."

I look at PhD hoping she'll agree but she says, "The chances of us outsmarting and beating an ancient spirit, demon, maybe even a god, are pretty low. That might be our best option."

"Fuck that, PhD! No way!" I shoot back. "We are finding a way out of this hotel and I am saving Wrath.

"Wrath is probably dead," Janet says, with an uncharacteristic touch of sadness.

"He's not dead," I say. "This is a game. Ok, this is a game that Alû wants to play with us. This is a draft. This 'thing,' demon, whatever the fuck he is, uses our genre to take souls. He got Shira to get to all of us here. He wants the challenge. He gets off on it or else he'd just take us. No, it's a fucking game and I think we can win, we have to. I don't want to be a fucking priestess."

PhD nods and said, "The game thing is true. I'm remembering more, now...Alû would want the best lullaby tellers to be sacrificed to him, but they could have a chance to survive the designs, mazes, and lands inspired by their stories. It all seemed like such a far-fetched myth."

"Lullabiers?" Nora says shaking her head. "He's a fucking man-baby demon. Jesus fucking Christ, I will never be a priestess for that."

"Has anyone ever stopped him?" I ask.

"I don't know, probably not," PhD says.

Nora looks at me and says, "Then we have to be the ones."

I nod and say, "We have to."

Janet nods. "Look, the odds are so low that we live through this. But if there is a contract on what your souls get, I could look at it and see if I can bargain with Alû."

"Oh my fucking god!" I scream in frustration. "No, Janet."

"He's a demon who wants to dominate women. Priestess probably means we'd get the most horrific attention and torture, or be doing the torturing," Nora says.

"You're probably right," Janet nodded. "Demons, publishers, they are just trying to screw you in different ways...fine, let's stay the path and work together and try to escape and beat this Alû."

We all nod, a silent promise to work together and somehow survive this.

Nora and I look out into the New Orleans second floor. Cajun music plays louder, a song of horns and bells that feels haunting but inviting reaches our ears.

"I don't care for most of your books," Nora says, "and I *really* don't care for this one. I hate New Orleans too." I glare at her. She takes a deep breath.

"This is your world Autumn, lead the way."

We enter the world.

The lights dance and sparkle like I imagine they would in the Bourbon District. It even smells like what I imagine New Orleans would smell like. Beignets and spice. Sweets and sweat.

"Can we eat the food?" Janet asks. "I never got to eat the banquet dinner."

"I wouldn't touch it and definitely do not eat anything," PhD says. "I imagine that the myth of Hades comes from Alû. If you touch any of the forbidden fruit, he'll have you...he could be responsible for a lot of our folklore," PhD says, sounding excited by her discoveries. Nerd.

"So what we know of Satan is basically Alû?" Nora asks.

"I don't know," PhD says, "Myth and truth always get mixed up until you don't know what is what, but he probably has made it into all the world religions. The idea of a tempter. That is him. Desire. False words. The King of Lies. He creates fictions to seduce women. The witch hysteria in the middles ages and in America might have been fears for Alû...I wish I knew more, it's like all these myths keep competing and we never know which are true."

I don't really give a shit about the mythology and truth of Alû. He will reveal himself as he is to us. We will know when we see it. But why my books, and why hold Wrath hostage? God I hope he is a hostage and not a corpse.

It's like the part in my stories where I don't know what to do but I keep writing to get through the chapter.

We walk slowly past the first street light on the bad side of Bourbon Street. Fortunetellers, bars, and brothels. I can hear the moans and horns coming from every direction. We are surrounded by sounds of pleasure and celebration.

We keep walking, searching for an exit, but there is none, only rooms, and black heart veins at the end of the street.

"What the fuck!?" Nora exclaims, seeing the width of the black heart veins.

"Maybe we should do the deal, there might be no way out," Janet suggests again.

I turn around and look back at fake Bourbon Street with the different shops. "It's a game. A chapter. And we have to figure out how to get to the next chapter."

"Ok,' Nora replies. "I get that, but then where do we go?"

"It's in one of the shops," I say, seeing beads and masks on the front doors. "We just have figure out which one."

"Well, it is *your* shitty book," Nora says with frustration. "I have no idea what the hell to pick."

I try to remember when I was writing it. I was marathoning it. I can remember the Redbulls I drank, but barely the characters, even the plot. I look at the room numbers and try to remember any kind of detail. I scan and scan and see room 232, that was the fortuneteller Ronvue's apartment number.

"232, the fortune teller," I say. "She should have the path. That is what feels right....I think..."

Nora gives me a contemplative look but then shakes her head in disagreement. "No, that is a bad choice. A fortuneteller is a symbol that you are messing with the fates. It's weak storytelling, no true causality. There is no power there. That's anti-Shakespearean, you should really read *The X-RAY Vision of Fiction*." Nora looks down the hall and points to room 252 with a happy and sad mask on it. "That is where we should go. That is the path to the next level, Alû is all about pain and pleasure, that is the path. He wants to be understood, he wants to know that we get what he is about."

"I think I know my own story," I protest.

"But it's not your story anymore, it's Alû's," Nora says. "Demon fuckedness aside, he actually reads and researches."

We look at PhD and she says, "There are rumors that demons inspired Shakespeare and the Brontë Sisters...and other famous writers."

"I don't care what X-Ray fiction or whatever MFA nonsense books say," I shoot back. "All I have is my gut and intuition and it has been right every time so far. I think I get Alû's plotting, so to speak. 232 is the right room."

"Fine," Nora says with annoyance, "but you're going first."

CHAPTER TWELVE

I lead the way toward room 232 and open the golden handled door. Wafts of cigarette and incense smoke greet us. The fortuneteller smiles at us, her green eyes sparkling under the pink lamp light.

She takes a long drag and exhales. "Well, well, Autumn and the other prophets of dark romance."

"This is bad idea," Nora whispers behind me.

I stare at her, she looks exactly like Madame Noire but lacks the kindness and empathy that made her able to tell fortunes. There is something sinister in her eyes that I never could have imagined.

The rest of the women come inside and stand behind me, hanging back as far as possible.

Madame Noire welcomes them. "Ah good, all of you are here. I have cards for all of you. Come, please sit."

I look back at Nora and she shakes her head.

"Oh Nora, no worries, dear. I know you too," says Madame Noire. "Part of Autumn's anger toward you is inside me, but you are welcome here."

"I hate everything meta, I truly do," Nora huffs, approaching.

"I do as well," Madame Noire, says, "There are those that come in for a reading, but they only want to know the cards ironically. It is very disrespectful to the fates."

"We all hate hipsters, let's get on with this, Madame," Nora says.

"Very well," Madame Noire says. "Let me show your card, Nora."

"Whatever," Nora says shaking her head, "as long as it shows us how to get out of here."

Madame Noire takes another drag and says, "We will see what the cards say," she lifts the card. It shows Nora dressed as a queen. She is in black and white but everything around her is in color, including animals that surround her, looking at her with hunger in their eyes. "Your booksmarts make you the most knowledgeable, but you can't see the primal and the colors around you, and eventually that will eat you alive."

"Thanks for the tip, but I got a shrink that already told me that," Nora says. "I'm telling you Autumn, we should go to other room, and we should go soon."

"Ah yes, Nora, so wise to the point of hubris. Which will you chose? The fool or the scholar."

Janet walks carefully up to Madame Noir and says, "What is the cost for getting a reading? Nothing is free."

"Free. Us spirit sisters must help one another," she says, smiling. I know smiles like that. They are smiles that hide things.

"Do you have a contract I can see?" Janet asks.

"Here is your card, it is the contract," Madame Noire says, turning it over. It reveals Janet — her face, happy on one side and sad on the other.

Janet holds it up and says, "It looks like the door Nora said we should go through."

Madame Noire scowls at PhD and says, "You do not get a card. You are not welcome here. Only one non-priestess is welcome. You have brought two to a sacred place. You as a group gets the card of judgment...." she then looks at me and I see her eyes go red as Alû's. "Dear Autumn, I expected you to get further."

She holds up the card and I notice how the light reflects off the sharp edges, sharper than a normal card.

Shit.

"Duck!" I yell, "duck now!"

I drop down and the other women duck too.

Madame throws the metallic bladed Judgment card. It misses me but slices off a piece of PhD's blond locks.

I look up and see Madame Noire reaching for more cards.

"Crawl out and close the door."

We all stay on our knees; Nora slams the door shut with her heels and stares at me, fuming.

"I know, I know, I know," I say and look at the door Nora had suggested. Since sobering up, my gut got where I needed to be, but it was wrong this time. Damn it, If I'm going to live I'm going to have to trust these bitches.

Nora opens the door to room 232 and my eyes adjust to the expanded size.

It's not a room but a ballroom filled with men, many of them. They are all tall and attractive wearing clothes from the 1700s. They are dancing with each other but there is no music playing. It's as if together they can hear a song that's only in their heads.

A few men in the front spot us. They smile and we instantly see their pearly fangs.

"It looks like a gay vampire masquerade?" says Janet. "This might not be the right door either."

"It is," Nora says shaking her head with annoyance

and disbelief, "I remember the vampires from your stupid book."

I nod, recognizing all of the vampires.

"What book do you speak of," the tallest and hottest one, Victorio says. Damn, he really is gorgeous, he's even hotter than I even imagined when writing him.

Besides Wrath, Victorio is probably my ultimate fantasy.

He stares into my eyes and says, "We've been without a woman's touch for eternities. Oh how ravishing all of you look. Let us bring you to bliss."

The pretty vampire boys nod. Their old garments fitting their buff bodies, their dimensions are almost unreal, like they exist only to make even the most frigid pussy wet.

Damn, I really designed these guys right. I can barely take my eyes off them.

"Yeah, well my husband says a weekend can feel like an eternity, so no thanks," Nora says. "Show us the way out, I know this is the door."

The masquerade vampires laugh. It would have been creepy if they weren't so fucking hot. The men step further and say together, "LADIES, WE ARE A GIFT. WE RESPECT YOUR BRAVERY, WE ONLY WANT TO MAKE YOUR DREAMS COME TRUE AND PLEASURE RAPTURE YOUR BODY."

"Nah, I'm good," Nora says coolly, but I see sweat dripping down her temple.

The leader smiles at her "You look flustered. Weak. Let us take care of you. Let us show you our will and our power...of ecstasy."

"Umm, Nora," PhD says meekly. "I don't have a scholarly solution to stop ridiculously hot androgynous vampires..."

Janet stares at them with a naked lust that's kind of

gross. "I feel menopause in reverse. Maybe they really are a gift."

I try to the observe this as a scene. This is part of the game. I know it. I scan our body language—it's timid and submissive, it makes the vampires act more dominant and sexual. The more we show our desire and fear of them, the more dangerous they become.

Nora isn't able to hide her fright and whispers to us, "Weren't they slaves to some vampire mistress...it doesn't matter. They're creeping me the fuck out. We need to get out of here, now!"

"It does matter," I say trying to be reassuring. "Every little part matters in every scene."

The vampires hiss and strut toward us. The leader walks with more dominance with each step he takes. "We will show you the way."

"Fuck," Nora says. "I fucked up." She turns around to open the door to get out but its locked.

I see now what I have to do, and I yell at Nora, "Stop, you just are acting like a little bitch." I arch my shoulders and stand as alpha as my angriest of my ex-boyfriends and turn to the vampires. "Stop walking toward me you worthless blood sucking little bitch boys. I said stop! You follow what I say!"

The alpha vampires stop and I notice their shoulders beginning to droop just a little bit, enough to show I can out alpha them.

They hiss with their sexy faces but I yell, "Stop hissing! Stop it, now! I find your teeth disgusting, you tiny dick demons. I am your god. Silence. Now!"

The others look at me in shock, but I own my alpha stance. The dominant leader stares at me and adjusts his cock. Jesus. I can see it sticking to his thighs. He grabs it. "Small? What a lie! You know you want to kneel before this and take it like a communion."

"No I won't! It is worthless. It disgusts me! Get on your knees and the rest of your losers follow. Do it now!"

The sexy vampires whimper. I stamp my foot and scream, "I said right now! Don't make me ask again, or you will be punished!"

The vampires close their mouths and get on their knees. I keep my alpha bitch persona going. "And you bitches, you follow me out this fucking door. And you bloodsucking sissy boys, yes, all of you. Open the doors so we may go to the next floor. Now!"

The head vampire meekly raises his hand and asks, "Mad..ame Autumn... may I open the exit door... for you?"

"Yes and then you can go touch yourself in the corner." I yell in my best dominatrix impression.

"Jesus," Nora says. "If we live, Wrath is going to be in for a surprise."

I give her a quick nod, but stay in character. "Silence, I am the lord in this room," I walk with determination to the door and bark at the sexy vampires, "Don't you fucking look at us! You are not worthy of gazing upon us."

The alpha vampire and his legions kneel in a perfect row as the door swings open.

We walk through and I see what looks like a staircase that leads to the next floor.

I close the door and let out a huge sigh of relief as my knees turn to jelly, adrenaline draining out of my body.

Nora smiles and says, "What the fuck just happened? You just out-Christian Greyed those Vampires."

I nod and say, "You were right all along, you just didn't realize how to talk to them."

Nora shakes her head and laughs. "I should have seen it too. They are total BDSM vampires. They will always do what the most dominant person in the room wants."

"Yup, I did come up with their backstory."

"Good job, ladies," Janet says. "Maybe we can actually do this."

"I'm scared to even see what is on the next floor," PhD says.

"It's the third floor," Nora says. "What is on there?"

I face the door to third floor and feel a chill. "The swimming pool."

CHAPTER THIRTEEN

I OPEN THE DOOR TO THE THIRD FLOOR AND SQUINT.

There are no rooms on this floor, but there is a row of palm trees and fresh coconuts on the sandy ground. It looks like a blissful beach resort. In the back where the indoor pool once was, there is an infinite expanse of ocean.

Shit, I can't see an exit in sight, just sand and ocean.

"What the hell?" Nora says in dumb awe.

I look back at the floor we left, covered in black gooey veins. I turn around to face the ocean and spot a Tiki Bar by the sea. I'm thirsty and hungry. On the bar I see piña coladas and delicious cucumber sandwiches, fresh fruit and decadent chocolate cake all laid out for us. I can smell it all and it all smells like heaven.

"Ladies," Janet says, in awe of the bar and ocean, "if this is Alû's world, this wouldn't be so bad. Hell, I could go for a piña colada right now."

"Don't drink or eat anything!" PhD orders, wrapping her blue dress scarf over her mouth. "And cover your nostrils, this scent will only make it harder."

It makes me feel full, inhaling the scents, reminding

me of when I first started drinking and fell in love with the after-scent of a stiff drink.

The wind from the endless ocean blows the bar aromas toward me. The flavors call and seduce me. Chocolate and alcohol sing to me. What does PhD really know? Maybe food is just a gift to give us strength to play his game.

I'm about to walk over to the bar but PhD grabs my arm and pinches my nostrils. "Hey don't do that," I squeak.

But after a few breaths only through my mouth I can think straight again and resist the pull.

Nora wraps her dress scarf around her face. "This is Persephone personified. All these myths we heard of, they are probably true and Alû's been the one behind all of them. We can't eat, fuck, or drink anything here."

Janet is the only one not covering her nose. She walks over to the bar like a zombie. "Nonsense."

"Don't!" PhD screams. "Janet, please stop! Drastic consequences will happen if you eat or drink anything..."

"Fuck it, there's no escaping this," Janet says, grinning and picking up a piña colada, "Cheers, cunts," and tips it back. She takes a bite of chocolate covered strawberries. "Wow. If this kills me, it was worth it. You need to try these, they are so...."

Her face goes red and she falls to the ground.

"Fuck," Nora says. Let's try to pump her stomach and make her puke."

But I see her body start to convulse. "Don't go near her."

"No!" Nora yells. "We can save her."

Janet's eyes turn red. "It's too late."

The red in Janet's eyes beams brighter. She rises like the undead and stands up. "Join me, ladies. I have her soul. It is home. Drink. Embrace temptation. Don't fight it, you will lose.

"Fuck you!" Nora says, "Making my agent a fucking demon through chocolate cake. Fuck you!"

Janet's face contorts and twists like Alû is leaving her body. Her skin begins to melt off and her own eyes return. There is so much pain in her eyes, pain I wouldn't wish on anyone.

Her jaw falls off. She gasps, "he...he...eelp meee..." she melts down into a blob but I still see her eyes and a mouth.

"I'm so hungry. I have to eat to make the pain go away," the blob-like Janet says, swimming toward us.

"Oh fuck...," I jump as the goo that once was Janet swooshes up to me.

I run to the bar, screaming, "Get on top of the bar. Don't get any of it on you."

We hop onto the bar, standing on the top, feeling like we are in a really fucked up sequel to *Coyote Ugly*.

The Janet blob tries to slither up the mahogany bar, but can't get a grip, "Come down. Please. The pain! I'm so hungry," her teeth chatter while the goo inside of her squishes around on the floor.

"She doesn't deserve this, this is so fucked," Nora cries out.

"Here," I kick some quesadillas in the direction of her blob form.

Her blob-self absorbs the food until it's gone and bubbles start popping up on her surface.

I kick more food and alcohol to her and the bubbles get bigger. "Kick all the food over to her!"

We clumsily kick all the giant piles of food onto the Janet blob, until the bubbles look like they are going to pop and I say, "Get behind and under the bar."

We duck under, hearing a grenade sounding blast, followed by Janet's screams.

We peek over the bar at what is left of Janet. She is all over the floor, turning into black sludge and slithering back into the hotel walls.

And just like that, Janet is gone, lost in the world of Alû. I want to mourn but survival instinct keeps my gaze toward the ocean. The sea is gorgeous but I know it hides something horrible. I get why Lovecraft feared the sea. There's something truly sinister about its size and its power.

But what is this all for: the pretty ocean, the exquisite food, the never-ending bar? What does Alû get if we show ourselves to be gluttons? I don't drunk-slut it up anymore, but in the midpoint of my books, the characters always chose a dark desire that screws them at the end of the second act.

I look away from the sea. Nora is crying. She's gazing at the vast and endless ocean, her eyes filled with horror and sadness. She shakes her head and looks back at the walls. "She's... fucking gone. Gone!"

I want to cry too. I see PhD on the verge of tears as well, but one of us has to be the strong one. I remind myself how badly I want to live, how I want to go on another date with Wrath, hell maybe even have a kid, maybe not.

I step over the bar and land feet first on the sticky and disgusting floor. "I'm sad and scared too, Janet...what happened...it's awful but even worse things can happen to us. We have to be strong, and we have to keep going. We have to win each scene Alû throws at us....I can't do this alone."

Nora wipes a tear from her face. "She was at my remarriage, she was at my daughter's graduation. She was there for me. She was a cunt but she was my cunt. She was even one my bridesmaids, and now she's just gone..."

"I know, I know," I say, trying to comfort her. "I really believe if all three of us watch each other's backs and work together, we will survive. Hours ago, we all hated each other, but now we need each other, and we need to get the fuck out of here."

Nora and PhD nod their heads.

We hear the sound of a ship's horn and look out to sea.

A deep operatic voice bellows, "Ahoy, my beauties."

Nora squints and sighs. "You got to be kidding me, a fucking merman!"

CHAPTER FOURTEEN

On a luxurious yacht is a tan, tall gorgeous man, standing proudly on the tip of his mermaid tail.

And of course, I recognize him. "*Shipwrecked Siren*," I say in disbelief. "One of my least favorite books."

"I liked it," PhD says. "There aren't many merman and siren love stories."

"We are going to need that boat," I say, recalling some of the plot. "It's the only way out. We are the sirens."

Nora shakes her head and rolls her eyes. "Of course it is."

The merman stares at us and smiles. "Ahoy, my beauties. Though you are all enchanting, only one of you can be a siren and reach the other shore. The chosen one will be treated like a princess on my yacht. The others shall drown and be swallowed into the sea."

"Why does he sound like a fired actor from a renaissance fair?" Nora asks. "And seriously, the merman owns a yacht. That's just fucking trite, Autumn."

"Shut up," I say, trying to remember how I even came up with this silly book idea. I think it was just wanting to go on a beach vacation and not able to afford one. It was plain old wish fulfillment. At least it made some money.

I stare at him and remember that sand was the only thing that could cool his lust. Why? Hell if I know, probably to make the stupid plot work, but it made sense at the time.

"Fine," I say, scared, but trusting my grasp of the scene, "Come down, and choose."

"I am not one for land," he scoffs.

"Then you will get none of us," I respond.

"What the fuck are you doing?" Nora whispers.

"Letting him choose, trust me," I whisper.

"Very well," he says, looking us over like sushi rolls on a plate.

He leaps into the ocean and wades through the water until he's as close as he can get to land.

I stretch my heel and kick the sand as hard as I can. I scream, "Kick and scoop! Do it!"

"No!" the merman screams, but the others follow my lead. Sand flies at him as he hisses and screams.

He tries to turn around and go back to his yacht, but the sand turns into cement when it hits his body.

We keep kicking and throwing sand. He hisses and screams when the cement hits his tail, sticking to it and hardening onto it.

"Kick and swat faster and harder!" I say, out of breath.

Nora grabs a bath bomb amount and tosses it right at his face. PhD and I clumsily kick more sand on him, it sticks and hardens until he is a statue. His hardened body topples to the ground, giving us a bridge to his yacht.

We get on board and the women look at me like I'll know how to start and steer the ship. I look cluelessly at the steering wheel, realizing that I've never been on a boat.

"This is your story, Autumn," Nora says. "Please tell me you at least researched how to drive a yacht."

"Um..." I say searching around the front, hoping there is a manual or something.

"Jesus, let me try," Nora says, looking around the front with me, but neither of us can find a keyhole or even an engine.

"Look," PhD says, "Look ahead."

I squint and see land and a sign.

"Do you see that?" PhD asks.

"Yeah, but I can't find a key hole," Nora says.

"Or an engine," I say.

"Maybe we are the keys." PhD replies.

"What?" I say, annoyed.

"Try to make it run," PhD says, "Use your imagination. *Will* it to be."

"Oh cut the bullshit," Nora shoots back.

It does sound like bullshit, but this world is built on my bullshit," I shrug and say, "It's worth a shot."

I focus on the wheel and where we need to go. Each scene we start will either lead us to damnation or closer to freedom. I still don't get why Alû doesn't just end this. Is this foreplay or entertainment for him? That doesn't matter right now, all that matters is getting this yacht to move forward.

Move

Nothing.

Move.

Still nothing.

Ok, focus, focus, come on, I can do this.

I look inward and try conjuring up that feeling and energy I get when I'm sitting on my couch and typing up a draft—fixing what needs to be fixed— remembering I am in control.

I imagine the wheel turning and the boat moving forward; the boat heading right to the tiny little sign we can see that leads to whatever is next. I picture more layers and movements until I can I feel it, until it is all real and I can feel the boat gliding.

When my eyes open, I see it is actually gliding toward the mirage that looks forever away.

"Holy fuck, it actually worked," gasps Nora in relief and disbelief.

"But where are going we now?" I ask. "What the hell is next?"

PhD stares into the fake sun. "If the mind is really our soul, or vice versa, he's testing ours. I just wish I knew why."

The thought makes me shiver. Alû reminds me of so many shitty guys I've met at bars, they always put you through these sadistic tests, and half of them don't even want to be with you after you fuck. I used to think there was something wrong with men, but now I wonder how much Alû has influenced them too.

The wind gets colder the further out we get. It's all starting to feel a little too real, maybe this is what virtual reality will feel like when it's perfected. I don't like that I'm starting loose my sense of what is real, and I worry that could be part of his master plan.

The water that looks more like a lake than an ocean now. It's so clear I can see my reflection and Nora's. Wow, I look like shit. I rub underneath my eyes but see my reflection look up and smile at me. Nora's reflection grabs my reflections hair and begins choking me.

"You are killing me," I say, feeling scared. "I hope it's not prophecy."

"You're doing worse to me, honey," Nora shoots back, looking away from the sea.

"Don't look at the water," I hear PhD saying, forcing herself to look away. "It's awful.. He's playing with us."

I worry that the ocean water is foreshadowing something, and I keep my eye on Nora. She places her arm on my shoulder and cringe and jump. "Relax, Autumn, it's just me. Just steer straight, we are almost there. We've got to do this together."

I nod but I have trouble trusting her, it's hard to trust anyone. I force my eyes to focus until we all see an island on the horizon.

It looks so real. A jungle, but more than that, its geology doesn't look like it's from any time I've ever seen or learned about in history books. It looks like a time before humans. It's epic, going for miles and miles, but right up ahead stands a door, just like the ones at the hotel that says,

4th Floor.

CHAPTER FIFTEEN

We make it to shore and stare at the disconcerting door.

"The door looks like the cover of *Intro to Existentialism*, a book I read in college," PhD says.

"You want to open it, PhD? Cause I'm not touching it."

"Nope," PhD says.

They both stare at me and I shake my head. "Fine."

I push the tall grass away from my face and walk to the door. There's no knob, so I push. It creaks open and the same tall grass is there but the terrain looks completely untouched by humanity. But it's more than that, it looks like land that hasn't been tainted by the last 65 million years.

We stare in awe at nature in its most pristine state. There are babbling streams everywhere, and behind them a volcano is blowing giant billows of thick black smoke.

"It's like something out of a science book of prehistoric times," PhD says.

"I don't know... this looks the setting of the Scientology creation story...I experimented with it in the 80s," Nora says. "We better not have to seduce Xenu."

I scan the area and feel relief that I never once wrote Scientology erotica, but it does looks familiar—that's why the books melted into the wall...but why mine?

"These are all my settings," I say. "All my characters, all the settings, but I don't even know what this is, yet I know this place."

Nora looks at me contemplatively. "I don't remember reading any book of yours like this, and I've read all..." she stops realizing what she is admitting.

"I thought you said you only read two of my books."

"Whatever, I lied. You are good at plot, I care about craft so I even read your garbage. But I don't remember any pre-historic dinosaur times."

My eyes widen and I feel nauseous. I shake my head and say, "Oh fuck. Oh fuck me, god damn it!"

"What?" asks PhD.

A loud roar shatters the silence, and the ground shakes from the vibration.

"What the hell was that? What the fuck now!" Nora yelps. "What the fuck did you write, Autumn?"

I cringe and shake my head. "I did it under a pen name,..." the echo of the beastly scream comes back. "I wrote one of those dinosaur erotica kindle singles and published it as a chapbook on KDP. Only my super hard-core fans know about it. One fan brought it for me to sign..."

Nora gives me a death glare. "You dumb fucking hack cunt. You wrote about women fucking dinosaurs and now what, we are going to have to battle brontosauruses with boners."

I let out a huge breath of frustration. "They weren't alpha enough, the brontosaurus. So I wrote about Raptors and T-Rexes."

"Well, Autumn, I never even contemplated writing Jurassic Park slash fic. So I don't know what to do here!" Nora yells.

PhD shrugs and says, "I studied paranormal romance, not paleontology."

I panic-scan through the tall thick grasses. It gives me cover but makes it tough to see if anything is coming our way. It's just wilderness, but I keep looking until I see a patch of blackness clashing with all the green— a cave opening.

Oh damn, that's right, the protagonist of *Testosterone Rex*, Charabook, lived in a cave. She was her tribes' artist and spent her time alone decorating the cave. I remember joking that she was the first interior designer. The men would bring back food for sex, but she never found the sex very satisfying. Charabook left her cage to meet the alpha male T-Rex. He pinned her down but did not eat her, well not for food. It was the worst thing I ever wrote, but it still paid the rent for a few months until readers moved on from dinosaurs to other, stranger fetishes.

"If anything or anyone can help us, it is going to be in that cave."

Nora shakes her head. "I'm claustrophobic. No, I don't like this idea at all...I can't go in there."

I do my best to give her a look of comfort but say sternly, "Nora, we are facing off against an ancient demon who has probably influenced our ideas of Satan and Hell. You can deal with a few tight spaces."

PhD says, "This probably *is* Hell."

"Probably," I say, "but I'd rather see it as a game or book. This is the setting for this chapter, but if we win we get to leave."

"He's definitely playing with us," PhD says.

I nod. "And our next move is to go into the cave before we are sniffed out by a T-Rex."

Nora gulps and says, "Just hold my hand while we run, ok?"

"Ok." I give her my hand and take a deep breath to prepare for the sprint. I whisper, "On the count of three. One. Two. Go!"

I hear loud growls echo off the volcano. The monstrous vibration almost makes me trip but we keep on running until we enter the darkness of the cave.

"Fuck, fuck, fuck,' Nora says. "Give me some light. Please, give me some light, now!"

I take my lighter out and attempt to get a flame going, it flickers but doesn't light. I light it again and again until finally a flame appears and so does a wall with drawings of a T-Rex being worshipped by stick figure cavewomen.

Even with the heat of the flame I get chills.

I keep the flame alive as we walk deeper into the cave. There is nothing in there until we spot a large mound of dinosaur eggs. Behind the eggs we can hear the sounds of human moans and they do not sound like moans of pleasure.

I look closer and see women's faces. Oh god, one is Janet, she is dressed as a cavewoman and is dirty as one too. There are other women with her that I recognize: agents and editors that were at the pitch sessions.

What the fuck?

Is this really Janet?

"Janet, how?" Nora exclaims, sounding both happy and frightened, "Is it really you?"

Janet and the other agents and editors look at us, but they look like they're something other than alive.

"It's me," Janet says. Her voice is hollow, lost. "It feels like I have been here thousands of years...so much pain, so much horror, but now that you've come you can be his food."

Nora looks back at me and says, "You fucked up again, Autumn. You fucked up bad!"

Janet smiles cruelly as she and other captives chant, "Fresh meat, fresh meat, fresh meat for the beast!"

CHAPTER SIXTEEN

Janet and the cavewomen pick up spears lying against the wall. They continue chanting, adding a boom sound, smacking their spears against the ground.

"Oh fuck, I messed up." I whisper to myself, as we walk backwards toward the light.

Janet and the other women don't chase us but keep chanting and stomping on the soft earth ground. I feel the hot sun on the back of my neck and all the hairs on it standing up.

We back out of the cave, but I can no longer feel the hot sun. Instead I feel putrid wind whooshing from behind...oh no....

I hear a growl and hot breath that almost knocks me over. Janet and the other cavewomen get on the ground and kneel. I know exactly what is behind me.

Janet smiles and says, "We are toys for him. It is miserable, but with you here—we can finally get some peace." She extends her neck looking up and says, "Fresh meat, my lord."

Her smile fades into fright and screams when the head of a T-Rex reaches past us. He open his mouth wide and chomps—devouring her entire body in one bite.

The other women bow to him and hold out their swords, so we can't run back in the cave.

The T-Rex lifts his head and stares at us. He's huge. A 100- feet tall, wearing a golden crown on his head and a tuxedo. He looks exactly like the terrible cover art I found on DeviantArt. I can remember laughing for 10 minutes straight about the cover, but seeing a tuxedo crowned T-Rex in the flesh is terrifying.

He looks down at us. I close my eyes and think how sad it would be to die being eaten by dinosaur while shitting in his mouth, but he just smells us and speaks to the women behind us, "Old meat toys, show new meat toys how to play with T-Rex."

They disrobe their scrappy decrepit outfits, and we watch in horror as they start performing acts of foreplay on the T-Rex. His oversized colocha erect, the women kissing his little arms.

"Ugh, what the fuck... Nora says in shock. "This is so wrong."

"The tribe became sexual slave acrobat toys," I say, reddening with shame, watching them swing to different parts of the T-Rex's body. One of the women gets near his face and cries in horror as he puts her in his mouth and starts sucking on her like she is a breath mint.

He spits the woman out and plays with her body like a cat, throwing her back and forth with the talons of his feet.

"He is a sadist T-Rex. What can I say? I was reading *Fifty Shades* at the time."

I turn away in horror. PhD vomits.

"Bored!" the T-Rex screams. "Want new toys, make love and food with them, make women wine juice with old toys," theT-Rex starts stomping on the women.

"Run!!!" I scream.

I'm losing my breath, sprinting as the T-Rex laughs and trots calmly toward us. Damn it, I remember writing that he likes to chase his 'sex toys' like a kitten stalking a ball of yarn. His massive size allows him go at a steady pace behind us.

He's playing with us, he could easily eat and kill all of us in a matter of seconds.

Shit, shit, shit, I gotta think of something, cause I am not getting sexually assaulted by a fucking T-Rex! I'm not going out like that!

Think, Autumn, think…all I can do is run, but then I remember there is a river nearby.

Nora and PhD follow me, but my hopes for safety are gone when I see pack of raptors in front of us. They are eating something, or someone. I look closer and recognize the 'food'—the bartender who offered me pills.

The velociraptors look up from their meal while the dealing bartender, missing and arm and a leg begs, "Please help me. They just keep eating me. My body keeps grows back."

We watch her leg and arm grow back and the pack turn their heads from her to leer at us. The T-Rex stops and I feel his breath on the back of our necks again, but his glare is directed at the raptors.

There are about fifteen of them. They break apart and make a formation like a group of cheerleaders. The pack formation turns into a pyramid, with the most alpha raptor on the top staring into the eyes of the T-Rex.

"You took the last batch," The alpha raptor says to the T-Rex in a posh British accent. "These are ours."

"Why do the raptors have British accents?" Nora whispers to me.

"I thought it would be hotter," I reply. "I was very wrong."

The T-Rex glares back. "I take what I want and won't kill you. That deal. That final. That rule of jungle."

The alpha raptor scratches his jaws in deep reflection, looking like the Philosoraptor meme. I notice the others look subservient. Power. Alû's world is about power and submission and to be best at playing the game of who has the power and how to wield it.

I hold onto Nora's and PhD's hands and squeeze them, hoping they notice what I notice—the T-Rex versus raptor power struggle. "I'd rather be with the raptors. I think they are way hotter."

Nora looks at me with horror, but I squeeze her hand harder and Autumn squeeze her hand again. "Yeah, raptors are way hotter."

I squeeze PhD's hand and nod. She takes a deep breath and says, "Ooh raptors, you are so sexy don't leave us to the mercy of T-Rex short hands."

The T-Rex growls and says, "I alpha alpha. I, T-Rex. I want. I take. No raptors. You no take. I take. Toys, shut up!"

"No please. Save us!" I scream. "I want all of you. We need your sexy bodies. T-Rexes have too much toxic masculinity."

The raptors hiss together and the talons come out. They lunge at the T-Rex. It almost looks comical, like an old cheesy monster movie. With speed and precision the raptors fan out, giving themselves longer arms than the T-Rex.

The T-Rex lunges with its mouth open to devour the top of the raptor pyramid. But the raptors jump apart like a Cirque de Soleil act—they jump back into one form and strike at the T-Rex's face with four talons and six bites.

The dominant T-Rex stumbles back and howls from

his bowels, until they move, and a mound size of shit explodes out of him.

"They knocked the literal shit out of him," Nora says.

"Shit," I say, looking at all the waste, "We got to find a way out of here now, let's..." my words come to a halt when I see the feces begin to move and a human emerge out of it...it's not just crap, it's Janet and the other murdered women remerging into this floor's world.

"Janet?" Nora asks, "You are reanimated as shit? This is some brutal Inferno...shit."

"Oh, dear, I'm so sorry." PhD says in shock.

The T-Rex is still fighting and bites one of the raptor's heads off. "Janet, please how the fuck do we get out of here? Where is the exit? You can come with us. Just show us," I ask the pile of dinosaur shit that used to be Janet.

Janet glares at me with her murky green-brownish eyes. "I'm stuck here. I've been eaten, fucked, trampled, and shat out over 1000 times. I can't leave."

"You can," I say. "Show us an exit and we will get you out of here."

"I'll help you, but Alû will only punish me more," Janet says, showing no emotion. PhD holds her nose while helping her up. "Follow me," Janet says, "but be careful, the lava is basically Spanish fly for the dinosaurs."

"What?" Nora says.

"Don't get any lava on you, ladies," Janet shoots back. "The lava is Alû's love."

We nod, grab her hand and run.

Behind us we hear the T-Rex yell something about us leaving. I glance back to see a raptor jumping up biting the T-Rex's right arm off.

We keep running behind Janet toward the volcano as it quakes. There's bubbling lava all over the volcano, but at eye level we see an untouched metal door protruding in the middle that reads in beautiful grey letters—

Fifth Floor.

"Thank fucking God!" Nora exclaims.

Janet shakes her head in despair. "There is no God here. Not in Alû's world, a world I can't leave. Once he has you you're stuck here forever, unless he's destroyed somehow. We are all doomed for eternity unless someone stops him. One of you must find away to free us. Please, you have to. I wouldn't wish this even on Jeff Bezos."

I wish I could take Janet with us or even hug her, but before I can say a word, the volcano erupts again and a drop of lava lands on PhD's left cheek.

"Go now!" Janet screams.

I grab PhD, who is walking like she is drunk.

We make it through the fifth-floor door.

CHAPTER SEVENTEEN

THE TALL GRASS AND VOLCANOES ARE GONE. Monstrous black trees stand lifelessly in a forest that goes on forever, but yet not even 20 feet away is the door that says Floor 6.

All the trees are burnt black. The smell of ash lingers. The black color matches the mark on PhD's right cheek.

"I'm not feeling right," PhD says, her eyes flicker until blood drips out of them. She falls to the ground. "Fuck. Something is wrong. I feel him inside of me. I feel his desire. His rage. I feel him as much as I feel...me."

"Please tell me you're not turning," Nora pleads. "Please PhD, we need you!"

"No, I am still me. I swear," PhD protests.

"Your eyes are starting looking like his," I say.

"It doesn't matter, I'm still me. I still have my will."

"But if you..." I stutter.

"Do what you need to, but I am still me. I am not his!" She screams.

I see a long piece of cloth from one of the cavewomen stuck to my right shoe. I grab it and walk over to PhD.

"Help me tie this around her arms, it's the only way we can keep her with us and still feel safe."

Nora nods and I give PhD the most comforting look I can muster.

"No please," PhD beg. "What if I...."

I tie her hands behind her back. "We'll protect you, PhD, I promise. This is to keep all of us safe."

"I don't feel safe," she protests.

We walk her into the char blackened forest, on guard for whatever lives inside of it. I look back at PhD, she is sweating and her eyes are reddening. "What are you feeling now?"

"Hunger. Awareness. And a connection to *him*. Truly knowing what he desires. It makes me want to be fully in his world, but I know he only wants to torture me. He wants so much, he wants..." PhD stops and tears of blood stream down her cheeks.

"Jesus..." Nora murmurs aghast.

"He is the opposite, the opposite of love..." PhD cries out.

"Can you tell us anything, anything that could stop him and save you?" Nora implores.

"I need to stop crying," PhD says. "They'll smell the blood."

"Who?" Nora asks.

I remember the setting now. I got a lot of complaints about how my writing lacked detail and people struggled to picture the setting—an ancient Viking country that was ravaged by war with the wolves, until the wolves and Viking became one people, one tribe.

"What the hell is here, Autumn?" Nora asks, the anxiety in her voice rising.

I sigh. "Viking Werewolves."

Nora's face drops in despair, but a smile appears on

PhD's and she screams, "I want them to brutalize me!" and starts howling like a wolf.

Nora and I look into each other's eyes.

"We can't leave her here," she says, but contemplates, "Can we?"

"I mean we might have to..."

"I want hot werewolf sex!" PhD cries out in delirium.

"Shut up, PhD or I will knock you the fuck out!" Nora hisses.

My gut says we will be stronger if we keep her around. I take off my shoes and socks. "I'm sorry, PhD. I have to do this."

I attempt to put the sock in her mouth but feel a large thumb behind me. Something that leapt out of the trees.

———

The sock drops out my hand and I force myself to turn around.

It stands nine feet tall, with so much hair on his whole body and an angry face under its Viking helmet. Its teeth are the size of my hands.

And for a moment, I can recall changing the channels and seeing a very hairy Minnesota Vikings fan in the crowd, giving birth to one of my most popular novels, *The Viking Wolf Who Whispers*.

"Viking werewolves, Jesus fucking Christ, Autumn." Nora exclaims.

PhD licks her lips and purrs seductively at the Viking werewolf, "Oooh, you're awfully tall and dominant."

It howls with desire, the sound reaching every crevice of the black forest. The echo lingers for a moment, but then a chorus of howls explodes and the ground shakes.

The world turns black. All the wolf men run from every direction, the white of the horns on their helmets matches the full moon. It almost looks likes leaves falling and blowing from the trees. I see more white when they show their white-jagged fangs, saliva dripping down.

Why couldn't I have just run to the fucking door when we saw them? But we didn't, and they circle us and growl while the alpha wolf stands his ground.

I stare into their eyes, trying to read them like a book cover. I look into the alpha's eyes and see the worst of man— the judgment, hatred, and fragility of men living in constant concern with hierarchy. The Viking werewolves don't see me as anything but what value they can get out of me. I created them after a bad date with a guy who looked at me no differently than the steak on his plate.

"You come from me," I say. "You exist because I birthed you. I am your mother!"

They howl, and the leader inches closer. "We have no mother. Women are food to be fucked."

Nora cringes, but PhD smiles and says, "I want to be the second option!"

"Silence, whore," the alpha wolf howls and says, "you are not my mother, because I raped her and then ate her. You are a liar!"

Shit, I forgot I gave him the most brutal backstory I could imagine and the Viking werewolves have codes that made them rulers of the charcoaled forest. My protagonist was able to tame the leader's heart through true love, but I don't see that happening—though I know his mom is his weak spot.

"I am the great mother of this world," I declare, "and we must pass through to next world."

"You are a liar," he shoots back. "I should eat your flesh right now."

"But you don't, because Viking werewolves have a code of honor."

"Jesus," says Nora under her breath. "This dialogue...ugh."

"Silence, stupid woman," the leader barks at Nora. He looks back at me. "If you want to pass then you know you must give us tribute. You must choose a sacrifice or we will ravish your flesh with all of our hungers and desires."

Nora looks at PhD and then at me and shrugs. "She's already gone nuts, and she is not going to help us get any further."

"Yeah, give me over to them..."PhD says, but then another part of her comes out and screams, "No, please! I am still here. Don't, please!"

I look back into the beast's eyes. I wonder if giving them Nora is the best option. PhD is half-here but right now she knows the most about what is happening and how to stop Alû.

Deep down I feel like there is some other way. I want to find that way but I think of Wrath waiting for me. I picture escaping this hell and maybe being happy after all this. I picture truly embracing life, and PhD might not even have that option even if we all escape.

I look back at her and see the blood in her eyes, and turn my gaze back toward the alpha Viking werewolf and hate myself for saying, "You can have the blood eyed woman."

"No!" PhD screams, but then in another voice celebrates, "Yes! Ravish me, boys. Set my inner wolf free. Lick this sexy volcano juice off my face and then lick me."

The head wolf jumps over to PhD and licks the black off PhD's face. I shed a tear and watch the werewolves run to the front of the door and block it. The alpha werewolf bites into her neck and I know, without a doubt, I chose poorly.

CHAPTER EIGHTEEN

THE ALPHA WEREWOLF HOWLS AND PHD'S BLOOD drips from his teeth as he commands, "Loyalty is the one principle we can respect above all. You failed! Violate their flesh then eat it!"

He looks ready to lunge at me, but right before he jumps he shriek-howls in pain. He falls at my feet and convulses while foam bubbles from his throat as he chokes to death. The other wolves who were ready to attack fall straight to the ground coughing and panting, just like their leader, until they are silent and still in death.

PhD is still choking in pain trying to keep herself from bleeding out, but her blood flows out too fast.

I run over to try to help her and hear Nora say, "Don't touch her. You can't."

PhD coughs up blood and says, "You bitches, you literally fed me to the fucking wolves."

"I'm sorry," I say. "I'm so damn sorry."

"We had to," Nora says, looking over at the mounds of hairy corpses. "We'll get you and everyone out of here. I promise, PhD. There is a way to undo this. There has to be..."

"Nora, my name is ...." but her voice trails away until her eyes close for good.

Nora and I wait for her body to be absorbed into the soil, but her eyes open blood red.

Her body lifts itself up, defying gravity and she says, "PhD, as you refer to, is no longer here, I thought I'd stop by and say hello, as you are now halfway to me."

"Alû?" Nora asks in shock. "You fucking bastard."

"Such a sinful mouth, you ladies are such naughty raconteurs," PhD says, as her face melts and distorts.

I recognize the voice. The cadence. The violence of each syllable and the sadism behind each word.

Alû replaces the body and flesh of our lost friend.

"Run!" Nora yells.

But Alû is already blocking the exit door. His tall frame and black cloth coated body leans against the exit. "My lovelies. So rude. I believe the look you're showing me is called—the stink eye. Language, it is such a fun toy. So are women."

His tall frame reminds me of Wrath, and now I fear he's dead. "Is Wrath dead?" before I can realize I should be worried more about my own life.

Alû grins. He mimes a square with his hands. A television-like screen appears where he made the square, but it has more dimensions than any iPad or flatscreen. The screen shows Wrath tied up to the TV antenna with his iPhone on top of the antenna.

I'm relieved to see his face even if it is in pain. But can I save him or is Alû going to end me now?

Alû laughs like he heard my thoughts and says, "I've studied you humans for so long I can read your facial expressions so well. So no, dear Autumn, I want him alive...for now, and no, I am not here to kill you—that would be cheating, wouldn't it?" he winks. "I only design the stories. I don't meddle with them..."

"My dear Nora, so quiet, so uncharacteristic of you. How do you like my living novel?"

"Fuck you."

"No, I don't think I will, Nora. You're not my type as they say. Too bad about PhD; she would have been very helpful as your journey to me continues. But in the end, she is quite worthless. She's no different than your machines. The tools of Morpheus. He's gained so much energy in recent days. But me, I've been a humanist from the first moment I've wanted to rule you all. The machines of Morpheus are little circuits of glory."

"So what are you— a demonic MRA talking about red pilling...Morpheus, what nonsense are you talking about? Either kill us or let us pass through," Nora says.

"Ah, anger. Anger at me that is drenched in melancholy. And the sadness of knowing your agent and PhD are mine. Though Janet was always worthless in this story, PhD would have been really helpful for where you go next. Poor choice, Autumn, but I applaud you; it's been so long since someone reached the sixth level. You got lucky, but the chosen ones always have Fortuna on their side. But seeing how the iPhone's powered by the energies of Morpheus has such power over people, I now want so much more."

"More?" I say, feeling a chill.

"Oh yes, so much more," he says and smiles with something that is beyond happiness. "I see how bland this world has become. Why should I be selfish and keep my story to the souls in this hotel. Why not think... bigger. So many lonely unfilled women in that little object. This Facebook, the bird of little words, flat pictures that are cries of loneliness...I want to cleanse this world of its sterile existence. There are many great lands full of ripe flesh. I want every woman to be part of my bible of desire. Where romance and suffering dance for eternity. That is real love and that is my own great desire."

I stare at him and conjure everything I have inside me and say, "No, because we will stop you. We have to now, you are not leaving this hotel."

Alû smiles at me with an odd sense of admiration and something I've seen in many men's eyes, a dangerous look of love. "Ay yes, that fight in you makes you such a treat to savor."

He moves away from the exit door and opens the sixth floor. "If you get through this one without your scholar by your side, then I'll truly know that you are worthy."

CHAPTER NINETEEN

I SHIVER AND HOLD NORA'S HAND, WALKING PAST ALÛ into the next world. There are actual steps and a sign saying,

Floor 6: Sauna and Massage Room in the Back.

I look back. The door is closed and Alû is gone. A wave of heat stings my eyes.

"It's so god damn hot," Nora says. "Can you see? My eyes... Hell..."

I rub my eyes and the word rings true. In front of us are flaming walls with a maze ahead. Whatever the sixth floor once was, it has been transformed into Alû's idea of Hell, or maybe it *is* Hell itself. Maybe it is my own. I don't even know anymore.

Each floor is more torturous than the last. This is all starting to feel familiar—not my own story—but someone else's. We stay in the middle and follow the flames through the maze. I wish I knew why this is so familiar because I can't remember this from any of my books.

It feels like when I can feel the perfect plot is so close,

but I just can't write it out—it'll come, but when? I want to tell Nora, but I spot shadows coming from the flames. Whatever they are, they give me the same kind of chills as when we first saw Alû.

We pass though them as they swoosh by fast. They got left when we go right. It reminds me of Pacman—buried memories come to me of dating a guy in my early twenties who would take me to this arcade hipster bar and get me drunk and play Pacman for hours. He'd always lose. Then we'd go to his place to bang.

Whatever is behind us is going to catch us like those damn ghosts always would.

"We can't escape them," Nora says, holding my hand.

We can't. They cut us off and they hover. We are met by two demons with monk-like robes that look exactly like Alû, but their body language is not like his at all—instead it is hesitant and meek.

I stare at the two demonic monks. They look so much like him except in the eyes. I speak to them like a hopeful prayer. "You don't want to hurt us. You are here against your will, aren't you?"

They stare at each other glumly. Pain and longing for better days echo in their stare, like I've said the harshest of harsh truths and then it comes to me: *The Monks of Darkness*, about two gay heretics in love who opposed a corrupt Pope. It was a short story that none of my readers liked, but I needed one more story to hit the kindle word count to make it a 90 minute read.

They still have humanity, I can feel it. "You were human once, weren't you?" I ask out loud. "You were monks that wanted to stop Alû. You've been here, maybe since the middle ages. I'm right aren't I. You've become what you've hated the most."

"If they are, they speak Latin," Nora says, "Let me tell them what you said."

"You speak Latin?"

"Of course," Nora says. Of course she does. I have never been so grateful for her intellectualness until now. She speaks to them and they seem to listen.

They nod and their faces contort like they want to cry.

The monks' eyes flutter and one of them speaks. Nora translates, "We tried to help the nuns, but Alû took them. They called to him, summoned him. We weren't able to stop him and he took us too. Now we are imprisoned in his world. We must torture his women for all eternity."

I stare at them and beg, "Please help us. Please, don't succumb to what Alû wants you to do."

Nora translates but the monks shake their heads and speak, as Nora translates back, "We were once monks of the Lord, but now we are Alû's servants. His heretics. We have little control. We only serve the wishes of the brother. He too is a heretic of Alû."

"Did they just say Alû's brother?" I ask in shock.

"Alû's fratis?" Nora asks.

"Fratis, si," the monk demon says and Nora translates, "The brother is the opposite of Alû. He is of the true love. He tried to stop Alû. Alû keeps him here but if the brother does not torture the women, he will be tortured. The brother cannot endure the pain. Alû is different. Alû loves pain."

"I didn't see that coming," I say, still surprised by the revelation. "Who knew demons had family issues."

"Shit," Nora says. "PhD would know about all this kinda stuff."

I can see the monks are losing control, they're getting more aggressive, their eyes losing their glow. They will torture us soon, but I get it now— the brother is the key. I whisper to Nora, "Tell them we will sacrifice ourselves to Alû's brother. We don't want to cause them any more suffering."

Nora looks at me like I'm insane, "Are you crazy? Let's see if they can sneak us out."

"Do it, trust me this time. Please."

Nora gulps, shakes her head ,and speaks Latin. The monks' demon eyes widen in shock but I see gratitude.

One says something in Latin and Nora says, "They'll show us where he is."

The fire maze continues for what feels like miles. We get to the center and I cringe, remembering another minor plot point, it was so forgettable and even criticized by some of my fans. Turns out the monks kept a minotaur they believed to be a demon's disfigured family member.

They kept him in a maze.

The monks lead the way and we follow them to the center of this hell world.

We take one last turn and reach a circle that has no flames around it. I peek inside and my heart stops. At the center of maze is a creature that looks exactly like Alû except for his eyes—they are a pale shade of blue. Kind, but full of sadness. There is no glee or sadism in them, only anger that comes from having to acts that go against every part of his soul.

The Alû doppelganger looks away from us and stares down at the monks. "You know not to bring them. You know I can't help myself," he says in Latin but in my head it translates it into English.

The monks tremble and supplicate in Latin.

Nora shakes her head in horror. The Alû doppelgänger leaps up with the same unworldly speed as Alû, and before I can even gasp, he rips out the hearts of the demonic monks.

They scream in horror but somehow stay alive. Their bodies fly into the flames.

I take note that having a heart in this world is the only way you can stay grounded.

The Alû doppelgänger eats their hearts and licks the black blood off his fingers like it's barbecue sauce. He turns back to me and Nora. "You are responsible for their deaths. You are responsible for your own now as well. I can't control this. It is how he punishes me."

"Alû?" I say.

He nods. "The more I see you, the harder it is not to torture you. The heretics' punishment is to be more like him, to be more like Alû."

God, I wish PhD was here, she could tells us what to do and what this all means.

I turn to Nora and she looks like she has more understanding than I do. I feel scared about to what to do next, but these hours have felt like lifetimes. My trust in Nora is all I got.

"You are like Cupid, or something like that aren't you?" Nora asks him. "You are like the opposite of Alû, you are love in its best form. I'm right aren't I?"

The demon's wings flutter anxiously.

"What happened with you and Alû?" Nora prods gently.

The demon still has a violent look in his eyes, but the question forces him to reflect, calming whatever control the world has over him. "You do understand. You must be a sorcerer of your world."

"I write literary paranormal romance, close enough."

"As a paranormal romance sorcerer you must know that there are energies active in this whole universe. My brother and I were birthed to embody love. But our ways to love are quite the opposite. Energies, like mine or the other gods...we need physical forms, we need a world to be fully real, or else we create our own...realms. We all desire to rule over your world and there is a struggle to be at the center of your world. To have the Earth be in our image and our essence is our real purpose in existence."

"I'm guessing you lost the fight then," Nora says.

"Yes. And he has banished me to his realm. Since I am his opposite— I am the king of the heretics. And you are correct, your idea of Cupid or Athena, it is of me, but that was many eons ago. Us spirits, gods, energies, whatever you call us, our essences still invade your world, and you call us, in how you dress or through the art you consume. Paranormal Romance calls Alû, strengthens him and now he wants more. I feel it, he wants your world and has quite possibly found a loophole to be the god of it."

"That's insane! How do we stop him?" I exclaim.

"You should worry about me first," the Alû dopple says. "I can't control it much longer. The realm drains me of myself, no matter how much I try, I always end up more like him."

I wonder what is the opposite of Alû's world?

What is the greatest act of heresy?

What is real love?

Nora backs off, but I go to him and slip my hand into his and say, "I understand. I do, and if you have to kill us, I will forgive you. But if you are truly made of love, then please know that I have a man to save who your brother is planning to kill. A man I could see myself loving. Loving. Real love. For this moment, be you, this one time and over-power him, because if you can, I know we can."

He grits his fanged teeth and forces out a smile. "I feel my real self. I feel... me."

"What is your name?" I ask.

"Qupaud."

"Qupaud. Show us the next door. Show us the way to it."

Qupaud holds up his hands and extends his talons toward us. Nora cringes but I stay still. He swipes down hard, not touching us at all, only himself—ripping out his own heart.

He hands it to me and says, "Where you are going you will need strength."

Before we can even ask what that means, he flies backwards and is swallowed into the fire.

Underneath him is the door to floor 7.

I hold on tight to his bloody heart and open the door.

CHAPTER TWENTY

I stare at the paradise that what was once the seventh floor.

I remember the brochure saying it had a snack area and specialized toiletries, but now it's Key West and for a moment it feels real. God, I would give anything to really be there and have a piña colada, but I look down and there's no drink in my hand. Only a pulsing bloody heart.

Nora shakes her head and moans. "Ugh, Key West. I fucking hate this place. It's full of STD's and stale Margaritas."

I clutch the heart tighter and stare at what looks exactly like Duval Street— main street, Key West. Every store and smell is exactly how I remember it. It's so life-like. Jesus, I'm starting to lose all sense of reality. Living in Key West has always been my fantasy.

I remember being twenty two and hooking up with some rich guy with a nice cock who kept saying how much he adored me. He took me down to his condo in Key West and bought me so many drinks and stupid t-shirts. We drank and fucked and walked the streets of Duval and took naps on the beach. It was perfect. It was where my heart felt happiest even if it ended with both of us cheating on each other.

"What are we going to do with that heart?" Nora says breaking the spell of Key West. "And why are we in Key West now? I don't remember you writing any Key West books."

I look down at the heart, it's the only thing besides Nora that reminds me that none of this is real. "I did write a book about this place. I loved it here. When things were going well and Kindle unlimited and other issues weren't happening, my goal was to move here. They also have really good A.A. meetings in Key West."

Nora stares at the heart and makes a squeamish face. "That's all nice and dandy, Autumn, but I don't know this story. What do we do?"

I look back at the heart and force myself not to throw up. Hunger is hitting me and I'm feeling weak and empty. "I don't know. I wrote *Zombie Daiquiri* under a pen name, hoping to ride the zombie train to move to Key West."

She musters a laugh, "I remember that book getting panned on Goodreads. Figures you wrote that garbage."

I'd roll my eyes at her if I was not exhausted. "Whatever. I can't do pure horror."

"How did the zombie outbreak start?"

"Voodoo. When I visited the Key West museum, there was a creepy doll named Robert that I saw in the museum. He..." my voice and body shut down as a group of navy men with blood and brains dripping out of their mouths stumble out of one of the bars. They are huge. Not an ounce of body fat. Their arms are as big as mine and Nora's torsos.

"Fuck me, I really hate Key West. I hate all of this!" Nora screams hysterically. "Fuck you, Autumn, for making me live this nonsense. And fuck you too, Alû!"

The zombie navy men continue unwaveringly

marching toward us. They don't move slow or brain-dead-like the way they do in the movies. They almost walk with a military-like swagger, a confidence that they could devour any flesh they encounter. They look so strong and brutal, and there's too many of them. I'd need super strength to take them all on.

I look back down at the heart and I shake my head, realizing what we have to do.

"We have to eat it, don't we?" Nora says, staring at the heart again. I nod, but Nora says, "We're really going to eating a fucking demon heart? It could be a trick."

"It is the heart of a god," I say, "and we must eat it to survive the zombie apocalypse."

"You take the first bite, and then I'll take one," says Nora.

I nod and close my eyes and I manage a small nibble, despite my disgust. It tastes like stale greasy meatloaf, but I feel a rush and take another, bigger bite. I hold it up for Nora to eat. We meet in the middle like a fucked up version of the pasta Bolognese scene in *Lady and the Tramp*.

* * *

The navy zombie studs approach us as Nora sucks the blood off her fingers. The navy men walk past us, down Duvall Street. The heart must make them think we are part of their world instead of the living. Everything is boarded up because of the zombie attack.

"Do you feel any different?" Nora asks, anxiously.

Before I can answer, I feel something shooting through my body. It's like a steroid booster. I feel testosterone and power flowing through my veins. Energy. Oh god, I finally have some again and it gives me faith that I can make it out of this fake Key West alive.

"Yes," I say, "and you'll feel it soon."

I look at all of the zombies stumbling down the streets, and remember that in my story, Robert the Doll uses voodoo to turn everyone into zombies. I wonder if Robert would be in the museum where I saw him, but that wouldn't make sense in this world. No, he would be in his old house where he lived with Neal, the little boy he corrupted and the first soul he conquered.

That's where we have to go.

The zombies are circling us.

"What the fuck, Autumn, they are not eating us, but they are sure as hell are surrounding us," Nora yells at me.

It looks like they we are surrounded by a white sea of navy men. "Shit, this floor isn't a mental test."

"Then what the fuck is it?"

"Strength," I reply, my gut tightening.

"Um, are you saying we having to fight our ways out of this."

"Yes!" I scream, stomping my foot on ground.

I feel the ground shake.

CHAPTER TWENTY-ONE

"Woah!" Nora yells, staring at the huge hole in the ground I just made with my foot.

"The heart," I say with a smile. "We now have the strength of gods."

Nora lifts her leg and stomps. The ground shakes even harder and a few of the navy zombie men fall down. "My god, Autumn, it's like we are in a video game!"

"I had an ex who played Call of Duty with Zombies. I based the zombies in the book on it. They might not eat us but they will try to kill us."

Nora says, "Got it. Put your back against me, and we'll punch and kick all of these fuckers out of our way."

I swing the first punch at a 6'3 rock hard-abs zombie that flies in the air, knocking down a dozen zombies. None of them get up. I punch another one with my left hand and it torpedoes into the others like a bowling ball.

Nora uses her feet, karate and soccer kicking with her left and right, aiming for the balls, rocketing the navy men into the air.

It works for a little bit, and we get some space but there are too many of them. I look for any advantage or weapon to take them out, but all I can find is the stoplight near Sloppy Joe's.

"Nora, we need to break apart when I tell you, ok?"

"Why?"

"Trust me. Just get across from the stoplight."

"Ok! Tell me when."

We kick and punch until I have enough room and yell, "Now!"

I run to the stoplight and lift it up. It takes all my strength, but I'm able to swing it and knock 30 Navy men zombies almost fifty feet away.

I hold it out like a baseball bat and scream, "I can't hold it much longer, grab the other side."

Nora grabs it. The stoplight spans the entire width of Duval Street. There are so many of them, but I can see the last house on the left by the ocean.

I yell at Nora, "Just run at the same pace as me, let's knock these fuckers into the ocean."

We each hold on tight to the pole and run as hard as we can, knocking them all back, pushing them toward the sea.

The Navy zombies and t-shirt salesmen are tangled together and we keep pushing. Foot by foot. Inch by inch. I grit and push harder until they all are in the sea. The zombies can't swim. They sink to the bottom as we try to catch our breath.

"Fuck, I'm already exhausted," Nora says.

"We have to suck it up," I say looking at the three story white house, "and go inside that house." That's where the doll and the door are, I just know it.

We walk into the house. The door creaks as it closes behind us. It looks like the house was built in the 1900s and is still stuck in that time period.

I scan the first floor. "We have to find a doll."

"A doll?"

"Robert the Doll. He's a doll that practices voodoo and causes the zombie curse; he kills and tortures all who stand in his way."

"So we are looking for a Creole Chucky?"

"Something like that."

"Why?"

"I think he's the key to all this in one form or another."

There's a painting on the dusty wall featuring a geeky plump-faced man in his forties. Sitting on his lap is Robert the Doll in a sailor uniform.

"Who is the creepy guy?" Nora asks.

"Gene. Supposedly Robert drove him mad. They keep the doll in the Key West Museum and people say if you upset him he curses you. There are letters all over the wall asking Robert to lift the curse. That doll has always creeped me the fuck out."

Nora turns her head away from the painting. "We have super strength, so let's just slap the shit out of that doll and get the key and get the hell out of here."

"Works for me."

A sound echoes off the stairs. It's like a creak but it's more of a moan. In front of the stairs is a man in a leather gimp suit. He isn't tall or big for a gimp, but he looks menacing in black leather with a red ball in his mouth.

"What the fuck?" Nora says. "What kind of zombie novel did you write?"

"A bad one." I sigh. "Let's just get this goddamn doll."

Nora leads and cocks her fist, punching the gimp in the stomach. Nora screams in pain.

Oh shit.

Nora swings her left hook to the gimp's face, but there is no visible impact, only more pain for her bloodied fist.

"Fuck!" she screams.

I run to help her and do my best impression of Karate Kid with a ninja-jump kick to the groin area. But the gimp doesn't move or even scream, and I drop down on my butt, the wind knocked out of me.

The gimp moves like a doll and raises its boot up to stomp on my head. Shit, Robert or someone is controlling him like a voodoo doll.

I roll over and he stomps his foot again, missing my head by only a few inches. I try to kick his head but my foot is normal strength.

I see Nora's shoe on the ground and grab it. I take the heel and aim right at the bulls-eye red gag in the gimp's mouth. I throw as hard and as accurate as I can and the heel hits the ball. It burrows into his throat, looking like snake devouring a mouse.

The gimp drops to the ground and Nora asks, " Where the hell did our strength go?"

"I .... don't ... know," I say catching my breath. I look up the stairs and say, "Robert the doll could have put a spell on the house to weaken all who come inside."

"So what? The gimp is his bodyguard?"

I shake my head. "I believe that's the ghost of Gene. I remember reading that Robert would watch the streets of Key West from different windows and would make Gene his zombie-slave."

"You think the door is upstairs?"

"I think the door is wherever Robert is, and that's got to be upstairs."

I walk up the steps. Nora follows. There are three bedrooms on the top floor. I check out the room on the right. I open the door and it's empty, I check the next one and it's the same. I go to the last room and it's the same—

empty beds and rooms that look like they have never been touched.

"Where's this doll? Tell me we are in the right place," Nora says, looking around the tiny room.

I look up and see a white cord hanging down, and smile. "We are...look, there is an attic. He is hiding up there."

I pull the string instead of arguing about the realism of my own paranormal romance hell.

A ladder comes down and the space above opens up. I can't see what is up there but there is some light from Duval Street keeping that attic from total darkness.

I climb up the ladder. I try to see the doll but he isn't anywhere. Nora makes it up and whispers, frightened, "I can't see him."

I light up a flame with my cheap lighter. The flickering flame reveals Robert the Doll, nailed to the back wall of the attic like a demonic child Jesus.

The doll stares straight ahead, not moving, but I can see a smile spreading on its cotton lips. I start to feel the bad vibes seeping into me as I approach his strange soft cloth body.

Every horrible thing Nora's ever said to me echoes in my head, along with every suppressed moment of frustration with my writing career. It all erupts inside of me, and the rage moves through my fists and legs. My eyes focus on Nora, who glares back with a rage that matches my own.

We both stand in a boxing stance. I can't stop myself. I try to turn my head back to Robert the Doll. I could have sworn I saw a doorknob under the little fucker's feet, but I can't look, all my energy is focused on beating the shit out of Nora.

"He's controlling us...and making us want to aaaaaatttttahhhhhaaaaaaccck...."

Nora punches me right in the jaw.

"I know...sorry!"

The pain comes fast, but without even a thought I feel my fist hit her right in the gut and yell, "Stop! Nora."

"You stop! Why did you hit me back, you bitch!?!?"

The pain.

Dolls don't feel it, but we do, and it's the only thing that can keep us in control.

I grab Nora's breast and twist it.

"You cunt!" she screams.

But I only twist harder and scream, "Do it to me, too. Trust me. Twist my tit now!"

"I'll twist hard," Nora says, shaking with rage.

"As long as we use our pain for violence, he can't ... ow, fuck that hurts...control us....walk to him..."

We side step back and forth. Each step gets us closer to Robert. I grit my teeth through the pain.

One foot away, and we twist harder, but Nora says, "I can't keep it up and I can't use my other arm, it will only... punch ... you."

"I got it," I say and inch my neck just enough to bite the neck of Robert the Doll and rip him off the door. I spit the stupid doll on the ground and feel his control weaken.

Nora spits on the doll and starts stomping and tearing him up with her heels till there's nothing left but bloody cottonballs all over the floor.

"Stop!" I say and point to where Robert was nailed. We see the door nob and the sign that says:

Floor 8.

CHAPTER TWENTY-TWO

I open a door that leads to another door.

It looks more like a gate. Behind the gate is a sign that looks like it's from *The Real World* that says 'Family arcade and Fun Time.' I vaguely remember when checking the hotel online, the Marriott bragging about its 8th floor classic video arcade and photo booth.

I push open the gate. Flashing lights almost blind me for a moment but my vision returns. I see a carnival. Every ride imaginable but no people on the grounds, I look up and see fairies flying around.

Nora stares in disbelief, "Fucking fairies, and my nipples still feel like burnt pepperonis."

"Mine too," I say looking up at the human butterflies that sparkle in the moonlight. They look down at us and laugh. God, I hope we don't have to fight the fairies.

"Hey, come and play."

"We won't hurt you."

"Come have fun."

They all laugh at the last line.

"I remember this story," Nora says. *Witches, Fairies,*

and Love at the Carnival. I actually thought it showed real promise."

"Really?"

"Yeah, I liked the twist where the fairies collect ancient myths for their 'freak show,' and though hackneyed, the romantic plot of the witch falling in love with Narcissus—who is forced to spend his hours imprisoned by the funhouse mirror. Your witch breaks the spell with love and marries Narcissus—that was pretty good."

"Tell that to Goodreads reviewers, they hated it."

"They're idiots."

"Yeah, they can be."

"So you've read it, where do we go?" I ask her.

"The funhouse, I'd assume. What about the fairies?"

"They won't hurt us, physically. They only do tricks and pranks."

Nora looks away from the fairies and I see a different kind of fear in her eyes. A vulnerable and hurt glare. She grabs my hand and says, "Carnivals depress the shit out of me. Fuck, I feel like I am about to have a panic attack.

Out of all the shit, we've faced..."Carnivals?" I say, surprised.

She starts to shake. I hold her hand. "Talk to me, what happened?"

"It's stupid....when I was 13, a guy I had a massive crush on fell from a Ferris wheel and died. I saw his skull crack open...it was a mess."

"That's awful."

"It was. I still remember crying and trying to conjure up his ghost to tell him how I felt. I wished I had said something and I wished so bad that he was alive still, in some way. That moment, that moment made me a writer. It helped make sense of it all...but here, nothing makes any sense."

I nod and say, "I know," holding her hand.

Through all this hell, I realize I've come to love and care about someone I used to genuinely hate. I wish we could have been friends from the start.

"We have both been through shit, and we wrote and created...narratives and stories to make sense of it. But if anything has come out of this, it's realizing that I need other people," I say.

My eyes get watery and my vision gets blurry. Nora is getting misty too, "I'm sorry I didn't reach out to you. I know how fucking hard it is to be a woman in this business. I know how prideful I was at your age. How I still am, and I hate asking for anything, ever."

"Me too. It's so hard."

"I know."

We are about to hug but are interrupted. "Hey ladies, this isn't a Lifetime Special, this is the carnival!" a fairy chirps, flying above. It farts and laughs. "Come into the funhouse and see who you *really* are."

All the fairies laugh and sing, "Go to the funhouse and meet your mirror/and see if you live through the terror!"

They keep singing that same line and I say, "We are going to survive this."

Nora nods, "I don't know if we really can, but I'll have faith that we can."

"That's good enough," I say and grab Nora's hand. We walk toward the funhouse. We reach the door and push it open while the fairies zip above us, manic, waving their wands and giggling.

The door opens and the fairies laugh and taunt us.

"You won't come out."

"But it is the only key."

"The mirrors make you look fat and say such mean things."

They laugh like hyenas and I wonder if this is really the exit, but the major part of the second act happens through the funhouse. I hold her hand tighter and walk through the doors. There's no other place to go but through.

The doors close and the inside looks more like an *Alice in Wonderland* Disney ride than a typical funhouse. There are so many mirrors, but they are not normal mirrors—they are liquid-like yet reflective. They remind me of the villain in *Terminator* 2, but they are even more menacing than him.

"Don't touch the mirrors," I say.

"No shit, Autumn."

I keep staring at myself. I look so different from how I feel. I don't see bruises or exhaustion. I look full of life, even happy. It's me but it's not.... *she is me if everything had gone right in my life.*

"Who the fuck are you?" I ask the mirror.

"You," the mirror answers and smiles...

The liquid metal mirrors start melting into the floor— our doppelgängers are no longer reflections, but three dimensional selves. The liquid metal swirls into different squares, forming a checkerboard.

I close my eyes and repeat the mantra: *whatever I see when I open them isn't real.* I force them open and on the chessboard I see six versions of myself and six versions of Nora—it's like the end of that Taylor Swift video.

One of my doppels, who is wearing pigtails and looking a little slutty says, "It's time to play with yourself, ladies."

"Oh yes," a Nora doppelgänger wearing business suit says on the left side of the board. "The game of who is the real you."

"I'm the real you," three different Autumns' say to me.

"You're not the real Nora," a Nora doppel proclaims and smiles.

"Nora," I say to the real one.

"Yeah," real Nora answers back.

"Grab my hand."

We hold on tight and the other dopples don't like it, booing at our handholding. The chessboard floor twists and turns and pops back up with the empty spaces now full of spikes and acidic pools.

The doppels stare at us.

"You know you hate each other."

"Autumn is so much prettier than you, Nora."

"Nora is so much smarter and talented than you, Autumn."

The chorus of negativity and shade comes from all sides.

I hold tighter to Nora's hand and ask the doppels, "What happens if we win?"

"You get the key to ride the ride of rides," my party girl doppelgänger answers.

"Yes," Nora's doppel says, standing in the queen spot on the board. "You get the key to ride the ride of rides. Pick who you should truly be, or be gone and replaced. One move on the board is all you get."

Nora grips my hand and gives herself the stink eye. "Bitch, I mastered myself when I did Transcendental Meditation while running my Milan Writing Conference. I'm getting that fucking key and walking out of here with Autumn."

CHAPTER TWENTY-THREE

I don't feel as confident as Nora. I drank to avoid myself and other people. All of them just seemed like distorted clones of my mother and her boyfriends. I fell in love with writing because it was the only way to be alone with myself. The characters always felt real because they had to be, it was the only way to truly grasp myself.

I look at them and wonder if I've become a terrible version of myself. I ask Nora, "Who should have you been in your life? Cause I have no idea for me."

Nora looks over the different doppelgängers. One who looks rich and refined but looks like she has never read a book in her life. Behind her is a simple woman of simple pleasures in a velour tracksuit, behind her is a spiritual woman with Buddhist prayer beads. The other is a librarian who has a look of contentment in her eyes. Another is a nurse with a wedding ring, and the last is a junkie version of herself.

Nora face's quivers and I imagine she's thinking about all the different ways her life could have turned out. I think about what she said about the Ferris wheel.

She finally lifts up her finger to point at the rich one,

but I stop her and say, "No, don't. Not her. That's your ego, go with your heart. Who you would have been if that boy had never fallen off the Ferris wheel."

Nora looks like she wants to pray before she makes her choice, knowing she could be giving herself a death sentence.

She nods and says, "You're right, Autumn. You're right," and points to the librarian with the contented eyes.

The floor rumbles and the ground under Nora's doppelgängers vanishes as and they drop down into oblivion.

The chessboard twists and shifts like a *Saw* movie booby-trap until Nora has a path to walk off the board.

Nora looks at me and mouths, "Thank you," walking to safety.

The chessboard floor twists back into spikes and acidic grounds. My doppels stare at me and I stare right back into their eyes. It makes me wonder if the mirror who talked me earlier might have been right. No drinking problem, healthy friendships, a good mother, and other things I never had, would have made me a better person—stronger.

The doppel who looks like she got an MFA and is engaged says, "Why do you deserve to live more than me. I could replace you and work with Nora. She'd have a better chance. Nora probably knows that too. So why shouldn't your best self be with Nora until the end? If you really cared you'd sacrifice yourself. You know I'm right."

I pause and ponder. This funhouse is all about self-perception and Alû is forcing me to look at who I really am. Every moment is a test to see how strong I am...I just wish I knew why he was testing me.

Yeah, logically, my doppel is right, Nora might be better off, but would she, really? Maybe my flaws are also my strengths. Maybe unlike Nora, I am exactly who I need to be to survive this world.

I look at them. Their strange hollow eyes full of fire. "You can't empathize with her. You can't understand why she needs helps. Why you need help. You never had to ask for it. My fucked-up-ness gives Nora and me the best chance to survive this. You are not real. I am. I am supposed to be. We are the truth and you are just the lies of Alû."

I look back at the dopple's eyes, they start to flicker. Faster and faster until it looks like they're churning themselves into nothingness.

They melt down and the acidic spiked board morphs back into a normal chessboard. My doppel in the king's position melts down and all that is left of her is a golden key.

―――――――――――――

I pick up the key from the glassy metallic pool that held my doppelgänger. As the mercury-like liquid drips off it, I feel its power charge through me. I've learned that in Alû's world, everything is a power object and this key feels like what I imagine a witch's broomstick would feel like, tingling in my fingers.

Nora looks at the key and says, "I'm running out of fuel. I feel so empty. In a weird way that was harder than all the other stuff combined."

"He's putting us through every test possible. I just wish I knew why. What the end game is."

"Fuck it, like you said let's just get to the next one. One more floor...that key opens something, but what?"

"I don't know, but it has power, I can feel it my hands. It will do more than open doors, but we need to find the next exit."

"Let's go with the fairies and find out wherever the hell that is."

We walk out of funhouse back to the carnival. There are now over a thousand fairies in the sky flying around. They look down at us, glaring at the golden key.

"THEY HAVE THE KEY."

"THEY CAN'T LEAVE."

"STOP THEM!"

The fairies dart down like a scene out of Hitchcock's *The Birds*. There's no way to outrun them. All I can do is hold up the key.

The key glows hot. Lightning shoots out of it like a wand and I keep shooting them down. I think about trying to find shelter back in the funhouse, but the fairies take their own wands and cast a spell on thefunhouse.

It shakes and contorts and becomes still, but a choir of familiar voices scream and it shakes again. Hundreds upon hundreds of our doppelgängers run out of the funhouse still screaming.

I point the key at the doppels but no lightning comes out.

"Shit!" I yell, running with Nora behind me. She is dragging and I'm searching for the exit, but I don't see any kind of exit. What the fuck is the point of a key?

I lead Nora to the merry-go-round but the doppels are too fast and are cutting off all the exits before we even get to them. We look at the horses with their porcelain shine and welcoming eyes. Nora tries to use the horses as cover, but I think they are more. I point the key at the horse hoping for more magic.

"Get on top of the unicorn," I say.

"What?"

"Do it goddamn it!"

"Bring me to the exit!" I order the unicorns and I aim

the key at them. I feel the lifeforce shoot out of the key, shooting straight in between the eyes of the unicorn.

The unicorn's eyes open and it growls. Its horn glows. I hop on its back. The doppels run at us, but the unicorn shoots bolts at them.

The unicorn runs to the center of the fair and I hear Nora scream, "Where the fuck is it going? I am going to puke if stay on this, Autumn."

But it only takes a few more seconds and the unicorn stops in front of the Ferris wheel.

I jump down and see a big keyhole to turn the wheel on. I stick the key in the hole and turn. The wheel creaks into motion. I grab Nora's hand and lead her into the first booth.

Nora cringes and says, "There is no door here. Where the fuck is the door?"

I look around as the wheel comes to a stop. The fairies are getting ready to fly and the dopples are surrounding us. There is no door to be seen, but I know the Ferris wheel is the way out. I am starting to understand Alû's ways. I get him. This level is a world of wish fulfillment.

"This is the door, come up with me."

"Fuck, of course it is," she says, climbing up on the Ferris wheel.

The wheel turns up again and I look at Nora. She's crying. I see in her eyes that she believes this is the end, she's all out of faith, broken down by test after shit test, overcoming the horrors to prove yourself worthy.

I look at Nora and say, "You got to believe. This is all about willing what is true. I see that now. We have to show Alû our will is as strong or even stronger than his."

She nods and another tear falls, eyes reddening. "Show me the door."

I wait for the Ferris wheel to get to the top. I know we only have a few seconds. I grab Nora's arm and say, "Jump with me. We have to jump. It's the only way. His world plays on our fears. This is yours...jump with me."

Nora gulps hard and says, "Ok, I trust you."

The Ferris wheel is about to go back down and lead us to doppelgänger death, but we close our eyes and jump.

CHAPTER TWENTY-FOUR

I land on my stomach, soft snow breaking my fall. Nora is on her side and wipes the snow off her face.

"It worked!" Nora screams. "Holy fuck, it worked!"

Everything is covered in snow except for a door standing mysteriously in the snow and says *Floor 9—the roof exit is at the end of the hall.* Underneath it is a no-smoking sign. I am ready to feel the heat and freedom of the roof.

Nora wipes the snow off her outfit. "Where the hell are we now?"

I look past the falling snow and see a mountain holiday lodge with a Christmas themed warehouse that has walls made of candy.

Nora stares at the Christmas on crack looking ski-lodge and says, "Autumn, please tell me you didn't write Joe Hill NoS42 Slash Fiction. Because this fucking looks like Christmas Town."

"Stephen King's kid? No, but I did write *Santa Claus Gets Seduced by an Elf Succubus.* It was inspired by the strange fiction of Robert Devereaux."

Nora laughs and looks like she is having a light bulb

moment. She taps her head twice like she misses something so obvious. "The last circle in Dante's Inferno was full of ice. Jesus, Alû influenced Dante. Holy shit, I should have seen this before...PhD would have figured it out 3 floors ago."

"More like likely Dante was writing about Alû."

"My God, Inferno was exactly Alû's world. He probably ended up getting Beatrice."

I feel a chill that's not just from the cold. "Fuck this, let's just get up that hill, and find a way out of this tortured realm."

We move fast to keep warm, and I wonder why the final world is here, of all places. Is it because there's an ice man or an air conditioner at the top, or are we really in the ninth layers of Hell like in Dante's Inferno.

Why take the setting of one of my most obscure stories, unless my stories tap into parts of Alû's stories?

"What?" Nora says staring at me, getting me out of my head. I gaze at the fake North Pole.

"I feel like Alû's an editor who's always going to twist the story to his ways."

"I wish there was an outline. I hate pantsing stories. Too messy, too easy to make a mistake."

"It's the only way I know how," I say. "We'll find a way."

We continue the climb. It's strenuous, but we keep getting closer, taking one step at a time. My eyes are tired, but I squint at what looks like a broken down purple car with broken parts. As we get closer we see it is actually a group of elves, because of course it is...

They are statue-like, but then the one in the middle opens its eyes and the others follow.

In my book, the elves were a type of dwarf that added comic relief, but in Alû's story world they look parasitic. They have hungry little eyes, but it doesn't seem like it is hunger for food, but for something much more.

Before I can get a word out, Nora shakes her head and goes off. "What the fuck do you want? Fucking elves, give me a god damn break. I'm sick of all this. This is so repetitive. I see through the bullshit structure, Alû," she stares up at the sky like Alû's watching, "Hey, I know you can hear me. You're awful, and I am fucking sick of it with this post-modern parody bullshit," she then turns her attention to the elves and says, "And you little shits, listen up. You're basically act one of the world, which means you have no real importance or power, so you are going to tell me what the fuck we have to do to pass you and you're going to tell me right the fuck now."

I cringe. I worry Nora's lack of tact could get us attacked before we even enter Santa's house, but the elves stay silent and the leader steps forward. "This world was built on treachery, the only way to live inside it is to be a gift or give a gift. What are your gifts? Or we will take you as our gifts to him."

I almost laugh, but the grossed-out feeling keeps me from laughing. I feel more annoyance and disgust at myself for coming up with such a stupid sub plot.

I lean to Nora and whisper, "I know what the gifts are."

"What?"

"We um... we have to ... give them our panties."

"What the fuck? Are you serious?"

"The elves, they had a weird ... panty fetish. I used it for comic relief. In hindsight it wasn't very funny."

"It's not funny! It's fucking freezing. My pubes are going to turn into icicles."

"What is your gift that will satisfy our lust?" the head elf demands.

"Can you please turn around," I tell the horny elves, "And we will each give one. It's a surprise."

The head elf nods and says, "It is customary in the South Pole to wrap them up or to give as a surprise. Very well."

The elves turn around and I pull down my underwear. Nora shakes her head and says, "My pussy better not get frostbite," taking hers off.

"You can turn around," I say and hold up my fist and signal Nora to do the same.

"Give me the gifts and if good enough, you shall pass," the elf proclaims loudly.

We open our hands and the elves look at them like we are holding gold. Their nostrils flare up and I make sure not to look any lower.

"Leave us, leave us now," the elf says as the others try to get a sniff. "It is up to the lady to let you inside the house."

We dart past the panty sniffing elves and trudge toward the top of the mountain. The snow comes down harder but none of it sticks to the top of the house made entirely of candy. The chimney is almost as large as the house. I figure that is where "Santa" lives, but when we get closer there is a woman standing in front of the Christmas wreathed door.

She is dressed like Santa with a full red suit and hat.

Like the elves, the woman stands still and statue-like, but I can feel her eyes on us.

When we reach her, she remains as still as a statue. There is a plastic-like cover around her and I know enough to know not to touch.

The snow doesn't stick to the bubble containing her, but it starts to fall harder. She looks like a human but I can feel she is something much more. Something otherworldly, not made of flesh like mine.

She reminds me of those mechanical fortunetellers that are on the boardwalk. I almost wonder if she needs a coin to answer, but the she says, "I'm not a fortune teller, but I know almost all."

I stare deeper into porcelain doll-like eyes.

"What are you?" I ask. "You are not human."

"I'm what you humans call a god."

"You are like Alû and Qupaud?"

"Oh much more than that."

"Look, doll lady, how the fuck do we get out of here and beat the shit out of Alû?" asks Nora.

The woman still doesn't move but her voice projects. "You act as if I care or even want to help, why?"

"Because this is the ninth level," Nora shoots back, "This is totally like Inferno, which means this is where Alû punishes those who were his biggest traitors."

"I was Alû's wife."

CHAPTER TWENTY-FIVE

WE STAND AS STILL AS HER BUT OUR MOUTHS DROP open from shock.

"Yes, I suspect this is news for both of you," she says.

"Damn, sorry about that, girl," Nora says.

"I am full of sorrow and regret at all times," she says. "I was his great romance, and when he was with me he acted like his twin brother Qupaud."

"We met him on the sixth floor," I say.

"Why isn't he here, isn't this for the great betrayers, if this follows Inferno logic?" Nora asks.

"His brother was just being his natural energy, but Alû was never being his. In the great battle to rule this realm, I abandoned him."

"Wait, so there was a battle royale with gods or spirits or whatever you guys are?" Nora asks.

"Yes, the fight between us 'gods' over who would rule your world."

"Wait, go more into Alû," I press. "Your relationship with him."

"Wait, I want to know about this battle, too," Nora adds eagerly.

"I was drained by him. His perverse views of romance and sadism, they were what you modern women call— toxic— but my energy soothed his. But then humans were born and the Earth called to us. Our essence being pulled down by different humans, and I saw Alû 's vision for this new world: feminine energies and rival men being punished and beaten until they enjoyed and accepted his *true* idea of love.

"You humans kept pulling us to your world. There's a part of you, all of you, that need to give yourself over to us spirits, to our energies. You are such empty vessels. You called for us, the way you call for a lover.

"Spirits entered into different bodies who represented the best of our essence. We wanted you as much as you wanted us. We used ancient humans, what you would call Neanderthals as proxies. Possessing them, as you both like to write about in your stories. We fought to make the world in our image. I betrayed Alû, along and with Krampus."

"Fucking Santa Claus?"

"He has many names. Alû has many names too. But Krampus and I betrayed him. We stabbed him in the back, but before he could be sent back to his realm, he put himself into the snake.

"But the energy of Yahweh and Evica, burned him and his ashes and essence went into the earth. Yahweh, poisoned Evica, double crossing her, becoming the soul winner."

"This is like Genesis," Nora says in shock.

"This *is* Genesis," the goddesses shoots back. "But Alû's energy is so strong that he burrowed deep into the earth and collected my energy, his brothers, and Krampus's, all who have the light and the love. He is the one energy that even rivals Yahweh's, and they've been rivals ever since. All of your Holy Books mention their 'epic fight', it's about Alû and whoever will have the power. But now, if he leaves his realm and goes fully into yours…he will win it all."

"We will try to stop him," I say, determined.

"A human will?" she laughs.

"So what's the deal, with Krampus?"

"Your idea of Santa is what Krampus once was, an energy that loved innocence and kindness. That part of himself he sacrificed himself to Yahweh, with his energy going into the man that took Yahweh's form: Atom. Alû took us all with him in his final breath."

"Wait, wait. You mean Adam, like from the Bible?" I ask, realizing how deep this all goes.

"Yes. The energy of logic and the energy of compassion. You humans think you are so complicated, but those two energies make you. We call, we tempt, we are waiting to have the next fight. But Alû, he has found a shortcut and probably a human host to rule your world."

"Wrath!" I cry out.

Nora shakes her head "So this fucking demon god or energy being or whatever Alû is basically a bitter MRA from Hell?"

"So to speak."

I stare in shock. "Why does he have you like this, why be stuck, basically in ice."

"Because Alû knows it's my greatest punishment, to be stuck in ice, when my energy and essence is about connection and being at one with another."

"Who are you?" I ask.

"Aphrodite, but like Cupid, I have many names."

"This is fucking crazy," Nora says.

"If we stop him, will you be free?" I ask.

"I don't know. No woman has ever gotten this far, but I doubt you will get past Krampus. All the goodness in him is gone, and now he judges all in Alû. If you go into the house you are almost certain to be eternally damned here."

I peer inside of what looks like a stadium sized home. It is Santa's workshop if it was built by Clive Barker. There are see-through gifts, all of them wrapped with red bow. The 'wrappings' are the same plastic that was holding Aphrodite. They scream through the plastic but I can't hear a word.

"How?" a deep masculine rings out, echoing off all the walls.

We look around but only see rows and rows of people wrapped in plastic packages like gift baskets. "Come to the fire," the booming voice commands.

We walk through the grandiose warehouse until we can feel the warmth from a fireplace. By the fire sits the most humongous looking Santa I've ever seen. Coming out of the fire into the a conveyor belt are the women, where he processes them as gifts.

"They never catch on fire, but it still hurts," he says. "You can burn in this world, but you end up being numb after a while," he adds, tying off another bow.

His shadow stands between us. He looks like a cross between Death and Santa, his face frozen off with a long white beard, hiding all the horrors of eternity.

"I must look different than your idea of jolly old Saint Nick," he says staring into the fire as a new woman comes down the chimney and is shot out through the fire.

Her screams are deafening until she reaches the end of the conveyor belt into the plastic present wrap.

He picks up a bow. "I only have to tie the bow now for his presents. Alû picks them. They are piling up since he is busy."

He stands up and sighs. He is taller than Alû. I can feel his power. He looks like an Old Testament god robed in red cloth and dried bloody skin.

"Us Energies... your world pulls us; they are rumbling, I have recently felt it all. A new shift will come, but I am trapped here. I still feel them. During Solstice, I feel Yahweh's energy. I feel it now, and my better self; I can feel it for a moment...but then it dies...It's comical, your entertainment, your distractions are so fueled by spirits, and you are making us more powerful. Alû found a way back to Earth and now here you are, I assume trying to stop him."

I stare at him and search for the goodness in him and say, "I can still feel some of that good in you. It's not all gone. Let us go through, and we will stop Alû."

"I have no goodness left. I am an energy of innocence and kindness and all of that I sacrificed for you humans. I was what you think of as your Christ. I paid for the weaknesses of your kind. I am forced to do the opposite of what I AM. I HAVE NO GOODNESS LEFT!"

"Boo fucking hoo," Nora scoffs. "If you want any of it back, show us the way out, and we will send him back to hell, set you free. Next stop, the real world..."

There is light coming from his eyes. "If you stopped him in human form, we could all be free. Maybe. Good luck with that though. He killed most of the gods in human form in the last battle."

"Let us out and we will," Nora pleads. "Give us the chance to try."

"You're right," the Krampus figure looks at me and says with sadness, "but not you, Nora," and stomps hard on the ground and a buzzer goes off.

For a millisecond I see that plastic-like wrap shoot up from the conveyor belt and fly through the cold air. Nora doesn't even have time to duck and the gift wrap cocoons her.

Krampus peels off a piece of his face with his own claw and uses it to tie a bow on top.

"No! No! Nora! No!" I scream and helplessly watch as Nora gasps for air.

I look at the fireplace and see the fire is out, it's the exit to return to the world.

"I needed to give this world a gift, to let the door open to your world," Krampus says in a somber tone. "I'm sorry, to both of you."

With the opening finally there, I can't run out of the exit— I can only stare at Nora trapped in gift box.

I go to her, choking on a sob and say, "I'm so sorry, I am so fucking sorry, Nora."

"I don't want to be trapped here, Autumn. Please get me out. I'm so fucking scared...."

I stare desperately into Nora's eyes and say, "I swear to fucking god, or whatever there is, I swear I will not let you stay here. I promise, I swear on my soul."

"Don't bullshit me!"

"I'm not. I fucking love you Nora."

Nora cries and turns away "Just go!"

I wipe away my tears and head straight to the chimney, I kneel, crawl inside, and hope this is the exit.

I jump up....

I smell the wet earth, more accurately the moist rainy air of Portland.

CHAPTER TWENTY-SIX

I land on my side, hitting concrete. The pain flows through me but shock quells the ache when I look up and see a vortex hovering over the entire Portland sky.

I'm back in what feels like the real world. Looking up into the purple swirls that continue to expand— I see the real world could be gone real soon too—it looks like a clogged existential toilet bowl. It could be gone in one flush.

I look away from the vortex and scan the roof. I see a living mural depicting all the horrors of Alû's realm. It looks like a moving comic being written in real time. I look past it and find Wrath kneeling down at the edge, staring up at the vortex.

"Wrath!" I yell, relief and worry washing over me as I run to him. "Where is Alû?" I pant, out of breath by the time I reach him.

Wrath stands up but keeps his back to me and says in a familiar and horrifying voice, "I'm right here, my love."

A nauseous chill crawls up my spine, reminding me of my first day of detox.

It is not Wrath. It's *him*.

Wrath turns around, and I see the red eyes of Alû. "No..."

"Aw, but yes," says Alû. "All those souls and the spirit of your award show, gave me the power to take this studly *moor* of a man. If I had him in the battle of the beginning for your world, I might have won the whole damn thing. I took him not for me my love— but for you."

I back away, but Alû in Wrath's body grabs my arm as I walk near the edge. "Careful my love, you've come so far, it would be a futile pedantic comedy if you fell. Not my kind of story, love."

Hopelessness seeps into all my pores and I say, "No," again wishing that the meaning and desire behind that phrase had actual power.

"There's that word again," Alû says, treating Wrath like a puppet. "Don't you see why I chose you?"

All I can do is say, "No," again.

"Yes, yes, yes, dear Autumn, yes, you need to see."

"No, I really don't."

"You are what I've been looking for, for eternity. My ex is such a...cold fish. I am sure you spoke to her. What a killjoy, for somebody who is supposed to embody love."

I cringe as he manipulates Wrath's face into a dreadful dead eyed smile.

"Oh, don't look at me that way. This should be a celebration. You are here, because you are the worthy one— surviving my realm you have shown me that you are my true love."

"What the fuck...me?"

"Amore Fati, you are my soulmate. Your stories, they called me like a bird calls to a mate."

"What? No way," I say feeling nauseous. "Why not just take me, why kill and take the souls of all these innocents, even Wrath, and poor Shira, you used her..." I start mumbling the Serenity Prayer, hoping it will help me somehow.

Alû laughs and cuts me off. "Ah yes, dear Shira, that foolish girl. I would have gotten to you but you said the mantra of Isis. You're doing it now, but it won't work."

"The Serenity Prayer?"

"If you call it that, I suppose, but it has brought me no serenity. I had to get clever and use dear Shira. She is the epitome of the human woman. Weak, foolish, and can only be whole with an essence like mine. So many lonely slags call to me, but they bore me to tears. My realm is full of what you'd call 'basic bitches,' but Shira gave me you. Look at her now, I have given her what she wanted— to be with her husband...."

The vortex continues to swirl. Shira is there, tied to a tree witnessing her husband being tortured by the characters in her own book.

I have to look away. I can feel her pain. A level of suffering that shouldn't even be humanly possible.

Alû makes Wrath's beautiful smile so wrong. " I now have a way for the Earth to be in my image, like it should have always been. Shira was so ripe for me, a vessel to get me to you. Her soul was already mine and will stay mine, but you, you are my true love that I've waited for my whole existence for, and like I knew, you would pass my tests and show yourself worthy."

I am in shock. "No, I'm just a fucked up girl, I'm an emotional wreck who started writing stupid stories to stay sober and pay the bills. You got me wrong, you really got the wrong chick."

"No! You are so much more. This. All of this is for you. It always was. All of these 'writers' are only dabbling in paranormal romance—my true essence—but you capture mine and vice versa. Underneath your stories, there is a deep disdain for women. It comes out so crisp in your stories; the feminine energy that always needs to be tamed by a strong sexy creature, but now you have found him in me."

"No, that's just my issues with my mom."

"No, your stories, they are the ones I love, and you see the female animal as I see her, as darkness that must be tortured into submission."

"No, I don't...not anymore."

"Oh yes you do. Every story drips with that essence, so pure; and when our stories combined you still conquered them. I finally found my co-writer. I've waited eternities for you. We can make this world into our dark fantasy paranormal romance.

I've chosen the human form of the body of who you have lust, love, and desire for. We will make our heaven here. You can have it all. But you must choose me, now. I am giving you the choice to cement our love...." he pauses and then turns his head back to the vortex. "Look, just for you."

The vortex shows all my stories and the women around the world that would be tortured for eternity using my plots. Men are there too, either abusing women or trying to kill themselves to keep whatever soul they have left.

Then the vortex reveals PhD, Nora, and Janet. Women I hated only hours ago, but now feel love and loyalty toward.

The feeling goes down to my gut, the place I must always trust, especially now. I feel my whole body flooding with fear telling me to run, but there's nowhere to run.

I look away from Alû/Wrath and say, "I will be with you and I will be your queen, on my volition, on one condition."

"Ah you learned from Janet. What is it my love? Name it and I will grant it and we will begin our union."

"I will be with you, but you must first free the women I was with. You must grant their souls freedom, and then I will serve you any way you want. That is all I ask."

Alû's eyes widen inside Wrath's face. "What an act of love. A little disappointing, but it is a flaw I can correct in time. Very well, dedicate your life to me and I will give back their souls."

"Deal," I say.

"Deal," Alû bellows.

He leans into kiss me, but before our lips can even touch his body begins to violently shake.

CHAPTER TWENTY-SEVEN

WRATH'S SKIN EXPANDS AND CONVULSES LIKE IT'S trying to expel what is inside of it, as Alû's red eyes widen he screams, "No!!! This can't be," his voice diffusing into Wrath's voice.

I push him away and he falls to the floor. He screams, "You tyrannical trollop. You dumb fucking cunt! What did you do?!"

I look down at him and spit, "You just agreed to an act of selfless love for womanhood. You lost all power by agreeing to that. So, you are actually the dumb cunt here."

"No!!!" he screams again and Wrath's mouth expands wide as his body shakes even harder. A sphere travels up his stomach, into his throat, and shoots out of his mouth like a venomous baby snake with Alû's face.

It slithers around. It hisses with hate at me and tries to burrow itself back into his realm in the hotel, but the top floor door explodes open as the vortex goes from expanding to sucking everything into it. I don't feel the pull of the vortex, but it keeps Alû's snake-self from burrowing below.

The hotel doors fly off and the realm itself flows out

from the hotel. The black hearted walls and creatures of my books are being absorbed into the vortex.

Wrath's unconscious body stays put but the T-Rexes and vampire boys float out.

Alû leaps up in midair and slithers around my leg and screams, "I will not go back alone. No! I will give you hell and Nora is coming too. I'll torture her even worse than you and make you watch."

I hold on as tight as I can but I have no strength left. The vortex sucks Alû, who is still trying to take me with him.

My hands are giving out but I feel the warmth of a strong arm holding onto me.

I look up and see Wrath by my side, looking down at me. He says, " I got you."

"Don't let go!"

"I won't! Are we high, as fuck!? Cause I'm seeing a fucking snake with demon a face and a goddamn vortex!?"

"No! This is real! Just hold me tight, please don't let me go with it!" I scream.

"Come with me and punish these pretty little whores, it's what you really want, Autumn," Alû hisses as the women's souls spin toward the vortex.

Alû expands and tries to bite Wrath, he misses but Wrath lets go. Alû wraps himself around me and I can see his hideous little face smiling.

I feel myself flying into the vortex. I close my eyes and prepare for Hell.

Wrath yells, but I know he's not close enough to stop me.

Something grips onto my hand, something much more than human. I open my eyes and see the goddess of the previous world standing strong holding hands with Shira.

"Thank you," Shira says, holding hands with the

Aphrodite Goddess of the Christmas world. "I am free. I'm finally free!"

"What. The. Fuck is going on?!" Wrath exclaims, looking around at all the apparitions.

The goddess grabs Alû, wrenching him off my body. "Love will imprison him," she says as she brings him to her mouth, swallowing him in one gulp. "You will live. Love will cleanse and save all who are in your heart."

The goddess flies back to the vortex with Shira, but her foot hits me in the head and it slams against the door.

I fall to the ground. I see them getting sucked into the vortex.

It all goes black.

CHAPTER TWENTY-EIGHT

I come to...in Wrath's arms. I can feel his speeding heart against mine. A real heart, his own heart. I look up and his smile looks almost too good to be true.

"You're ok... thank god, you hit your head and was out for a little bit," Wrath says.

I cannot bring myself to react in any way. I am too numb.

"What the fuck is going on, Autumn?" Wrath' says caressing my cheek. "The hotel...vortexes..."

"Is it really you, Wrath?"

"Yeah, it's me but what the fuck is happening? I think we were drugged bad, like this is some new shit that isn't even the drug market, bad. Like mass hallucination type stuff."

I look up at a sky, exquisite in its normalcy. Night has fallen. The blackness of the night soothes my soul. I choke back a sob. Alû is truly gone, but so are all the people I love.

A cloud passes and moonlight hits our faces. "Autumn, seriously, we got drugged. I was seeing devil type shit, and I feel like my body was somewhere else."

"You weren't drugged....It was real. Alû...I don't want to even say his name. He was a spirit or god...basically, a Dante's Inferno wannabe entity possessed your body so I could be his eternal wife."

"Aw shit. We got fucking drugged real bad," Wrath says. "I was smoking my cigar and then...I got drugged. You must have got drugged too."

"We weren't drugged!" I scream at him. "Everybody is dead. Nora is dead. Janet. PhD. All of them are dead!" I break down crying. "I tried to save them. I fucking love those girls, and they are gone. All of them are gone!"

I hear a laugh in a distance. "Holy shit you fucking bitch, you saved us. You kept your word."

Wrath lights up a flame from his lighter and it illuminates three different familiar bodies.

I recognize them all and leave Wrath, running to hug Nora. I hug her so tight. PhD and Janet are standing in shock. I hear Wrath calling 911 on his phone.

"You fucking saved us," she says, holding me even tighter.

I hug her back. "We all did it. We survived this. I don't know how, but we did it."

We cry and laugh when we hear Wrath. "Yeah officer, we definitely got drugged. We are up on the Marriott Roof. I don't know what to believe...look, I'm black, I don't call the cops..."

"Shira," Nora says softly. "And all the others from Con....they are all gone."

"But we are alive," Janet says, smiling. "You ex-drunk slut, you fucking saved us."

"You conquered Alû and saved our souls, something Dante couldn't even do for Beatrice," PhD adds in amazement. "Thank you so much, Autumn. Thank you for saving our souls."

I smile and say, "Dante sounds like another overrated

white male writer. Fuck that, we did this together. Us lowly Paranormal Romance writers did it together."

The moonlight returns. It flickers, and I see the mural below our feet. Aphrodite is eating the snake and all the women are eating chocolate with some very studly gentlemen who look to be at their service. It's pretty much what I would imagine heaven to be. I feel peace that all who lost their lives are now in Aphrodite's realm.

Wrath hangs up his phone and says, "The cops are coming..." he looks woozy when he catches view of the mural. "I'm fucking still tripping. I can't even..."

He goes faint and sits down to catch his breath before slumping over, passing out on the concrete.

"I don't know what we are going to tell the cops. They won't believe us," says PhD.

"No one is going to believe us," says Janet.

Nora looks at me and holds my hand. "We are alive and out of that hell, that is all that matters."

"Yeah, but she's right," Janet says, "No one really is going to believe what just happened."

"That's ok," I say and look at Nora and smile. "One day, Nora and I will write about it."

ALÛKNOWLDEDGMENTS

I first want to thank Leza Cantoral. There's something special about sharing what you love with the one you love. She was a champion of this book and encouraged me to keep writing it. There are some obvious influences on the characters, though we will leave their names out, but I think they'll see themselves. Lastly, I want to thank the muse. I really felt her guiding my hand while writing this book, almost like it wasn't even me really writing this book, like it was...

...

...shut up, shut up, shut up....ugh. fucking writers talk too much.

Blah, blah, fucking blah. Ugh, writers truly are the worst, am I right? Of course I am. I always am. Christoph and Leza, two writers and editors in love. How quaint and utterly boring, though these two remind me of what my dear Autumn and I could have been. What stories we could have written with the flesh of these foolish females and their mundane fantasies and desires.

Do you, dear reader, have that hungry flesh and want to be part of a paranormal romance?

Ooh, I can feel your giddiness. I am here. I am everywhere.

Instead of creating a new Bible of exquisite suffering on Earth (I have influenced Pinhead, I can say that phrase, he's totally my energy wheelhouse), Autumn got detained for two weeks with Nora and those other trollops. Oooh, but I can still taste their souls. It's a residue which I imagine is like crème brûlée on your tongue.

Humans never believe in spirits like me, hell, they barely believe in spirits in general these days. Conspiracy theories spread from terrorism, to spontaneous combustion, to mass abduction, that they were really a cult—that one makes me sad because we were a cult of love, but Autumn chose Nora and those whores over my love!

Am I bitter? Of course I am. What makes me even more enraged is after only one year, Autumn married Wrath. The wedding was an act of closure to move past their traumatic time at The Haunted Heart Awards. It was on the news and all these foolish humans moved past what happened. Humans are great at forgetting, but their nightmares always remind them of the truth.

Autumn did not write another paranormal romance tale. She enjoyed her time with Wrath and set up a Patreon account to pay her bills. Humans can be so giving, that energy of Krampus is still strong, but I can feel other energies coming alive.

Though Autumn didn't go back to her beautiful gift of telling stories that strengthen me, she and Nora rented a nice little cabin on the coast of Oregon to do some writing about what happened. Ugh, their bond and friendship is so disgusting. They basically had some ya-ya sisterhood time eating copious amounts of dark chocolate, defiling my good name and even stealing my own story.

What happened at that hotel was my story, and those unworthy women changed the climax and the resolution.

What an awful book it is. But humans have no taste. No real compass for great art.

The two of them toured all around the country. Selling their book "The Haunting of The Paranormal Romance Awards," going from state to state, continent to continent, full of smiles and tears, sharing their truth, just like Shira did.

Most humans believed it to be fiction, and many praised them and saw everything as a metaphor for something or other. Nora finally got nominated for a legitimate literary award. Literary writers, those of Apollo, saw respectability in how they used horror to deal with unknowable grief.

The news and the machines of Morpheus loved it and shared the story everywhere. Nora and my dear Autumn, believed they were getting their power back by using their gifts to share the horrors they dealt with that night, but they do not realize that the more you talk about me, the more you describe my image and the motives of my energy—the more real I become.

Traveling around the world with them, I see how far behind I am with the times. Adult novels are so 10,000 years ago and paranormal romance is very limiting, I need to reach the children. The Young Adult audience. They are the future, and these comic book movies have the power call me back into existence.

Little by little my image is starting to emerge, thank you Disney and all these corporations, knowingly or not making all these superheroes vs. superhero vs. villains vs. super heroes movies each month. Not realizing, or maybe they do, that they are making us old gods become stronger and stronger, and Yahweh's pull is becoming so weak that I believe I won't be stuck here much longer.

You see, on Autumn and Nora's last tour date, after another triumphant reading, they decided to check out *some YA novels. Janet recommended that they turn their hit into something a younger audience could appreciate and then have it become a movie. Though they were unsure of the idea, they looked through the section, but nothing caught Autumn's eye until she saw a prophetic title called* **Cosplay to the Death**.

Autumn saw me on the cover strangling a woman dressed like the goddess Iris, and I couldn't help but give her wink to let her know I'm coming back for her. I'm coming back for all of you...

And most importantly I would like to thank all the women who had a positive impact on my life. Thank you.

Sincerely,
Christoph Paul

AFTERWORD BY DR. CHARLENE ELSBY

Previously, I've written about the ancient philosophical wisdom apparent in the work of Mandy De Sandra[1]. In this new text, she's teamed up with her physical host Christoph Paul to bring us *The Haunting of the Paranormal Romance Awards*, and with this pairing comes an updated philosophy.

An up and coming author attends an awards ceremony for paranormal romance, and soon the paranormal becomes not quite so fictional. An ancient God Alû is brought to life and wreaks havoc on the convention. Autumn, her friends, and her enemies must ascend through level upon level of trials and tribulations in order to be freed of Alû's punishment, all the while taking the opportunity to redefine their relationships and come together against forces of evil.

The question arises as to what extent Mandy has influenced Christoph to structure the text according to the medieval formula of Dante's *Inferno*. I would assume that the similarity is a joke she intends to play on both Paul and the readers. The analogous structures of *The*

Haunting and *Inferno* is clearly intentional. At one point, Autumn refers to Alû as "a Dante's Inferno wannabe entity", and the characters discuss whether it was Dante who influenced Alû or Alû who influenced Dante. While the levels of hell through which De Sandra and Paul's characters ascend are not so cleanly divided as are Dante's (each level corresponding to a mortal sin), the levels of *The Haunting of the Paranormal Romance Awards* are yet all inspired by one mortal sin—lust. The authors' treatment of lust throughout the chapters brings into dialogue the sensual and the absurd, and we might even wonder whether the tests these characters are undergoing are some form of punishment for a sexual relationship that our main character, Autumn, begins early in the novel, with another novelist (Wrath). But I don't think Paul and De Sandra are attempting to chastise anyone for anything with this book. Even as the erotic creations of Autumn's writings come to life and attack our characters, there is no sense of a conservative bias against sexuality. Rather, the similarity, I argue, must be purely ironic—in structuring the book in this fashion, De Sandra is having a laugh.

The point De Sandra and Paul might be making is rather ontological than axiological—it's about what is rather than what should be. The writers characterized in the book move through a labyrinth of situations, drawn from the books written by novelist Autumn. Her creations come to life and, as the title implies, she writes paranormal romance. As she devises schemes to evade such creations as Bigfoot Fabio, S&M Vampires and sexified T-Rexes, we are reminded of Magritte's painting, *The Treachery of Images*.

An image of a pipe appears above the words, "Ceçi n'est pas une pipe" (This is not a pipe.) The image, and all other images, are treacherous, in the sense that they trick us into making assertions like, "That's a pipe", when it is clearly a picture of a pipe that we are looking at—a mere image, and not a pipe at all. An image plays at being real, and in doing so, it leads us to speak all sorts of untruths. The same treachery is apparent in the coming-to-life of all of Autumn's erotic creations, and her imaginations come to turn on her. Thus, when she wrote about raptors as potential sex partners, she relied on the image's treachery —the fact that what she wrote was not and never would be real. And from the reader's point of view, her writings are now being written about by other authors (Paul and De Sandra), and thus an inception of treacherous images comes into existence.

But the images which come to life for Autumn and her compatriots are treacherous in yet another sense. Besides being out to attack her and her friends, and besides being the creations embedded in a book within a book, the Viking werewolves who proclaim that "Woman are food to be fucked" are treacherous for the fact that *they weren't meant to come to life*. The objects of fantasy, of fiction, are a lot of times best kept in the abstract. We often fantasize and imagine things that, were they to become real, would never live up to our fantasies. As Simone Weil writes in *Gravity and Grace*,

When we are disappointed by a pleasure which we have been expecting and which comes, the disappointment is because we were expecting the future, and as soon as it is there it is present. We want the future to be there without ceasing to be the future.

As we imagine possible futures for ourselves, we must nonetheless fail to notice that when these futures actually come, they are very often not what we imagined them to be. One might pin all of one's hopes on a successful relationship, career, or other conceived existence, only to be met with a profound disappointment upon actually achieving said imagined futures. But the point is, it is not merely because the details differ in some sense from how we imagined them. The fact of the matter was, we like them being *imaginary*, and that is what is lost when an imagined future becomes reality. What the imagined futures have, that the real one does not, is precisely the quality of being imagined. That is to say, to make them real is to make them something they are not and perhaps weren't meant to be. As they come to life, Autumn's fictional characters betray her—by becoming non-fiction, a contradiction of how she wrote them. (A fictional Viking werewolf is very different from a real one.)

Another question arises. Is hell merely the coming to life of our own imaginations? De Sandra and Paul bring up this question in the text, in a conversation between Autumn and one of her colleagues, to whom everyone refers as "PhD".

PhD says, "This probably *is* Hell."

"Probably," I say, "but I'd rather see it as a game or book. This is the setting for this chapter, but if we win we get to leave."

The answer seems to be a resounding *no*. Instead, the authors point to the fact that our existence, and the novel itself, is broken up into chapters or phases. Each one is played to its conclusion, and a new one begins. The temporal realm in which we all exist is subject to change, and it is possible to change one's circumstance by manipulating the situation as we see fit. And this is another reason why the *Inferno* comparison to which I pointed above should not be brought to any definitive conclusion. While hell is conceived of as eternal pains befitting one's behavior, Autumn's ascent through Alû's challenges assures us of the effectivity of free will, the possibility of change, and the opportunity to be victorious. It is, in the end, optimistic.

The Haunting of the Paranormal Romance Awards is, I believe, an inspirational tale about overcoming obstacles, but obstacles of a very particular sort—obstacles which are, in fact, the creation of one's own consciousness. The novel speaks to themes expressed by Jean-Paul Sartre in *Being and Nothingness*, about how all of the obstacles against which we set ourselves are only obstacles relative to some end—an end which *I set up for myself*. Thus, the paradox of freedom is that I have the freedom to create something according to which my freedom is limited. (I have the freedom to negate my freedom.) The levels of Alû's labyrinth through which Autumn ascends are populated by monsters of her own creation. Sartre says that obstacles are really just "unrealizables to be realized". And as Sartre and *The Haunting* both make perfectly clear, the only real obstacle is death.

To desire is already to bring into being the possibility for failure, and yet desire is the human condition. The woman who wants nothing is no existent at all. (Desire ends at death.) As Autumn and her friends make their way through Alû's labyrinth, it is obvious that they have a common goal—to survive. And in Autumn's case, there's another form of desire besides—the desire to continue fucking a hot writer. She says, "Deep down I feel like there is some other way. I want to find that way, but I think of Wrath waiting for me at the top. I picture escaping this hell and maybe being happy after all this."

Are we all trapped in hells of our own devising? I think not. For the idea of hell is that it is eternal, while our sufferings, like Autumn's and her friends, are ever changing. Do the objects of our consciousness turn against us, creating our own unhappiness as we attempt to devise ever more clever schemes for escaping *ourselves*? Oh, for sure. But the moral of the story is, I think, one of hope and community. In the end, as Autumn says, "Dante just sounds like just another overrated white male writer. Fuck that, we did this together."

---

1. See my essay, "The Ancient Wisdom of Mandy De Sandra's *David Foster Wallace's Footnotes F'ed Me in the Butt*"

About The Authors

Christoph Paul is an award-winning humor author. He writes non-fiction, YA, horror, bizarro fiction, and poetry including: *The Passion of the Christoph, Great White House Volume 1 and Volume 2, A Confederacy of Hot Dogs, Horror Film Poems* and *At Least I Get You < In My Art*. He is the managing editor of CLASH Books which he runs with his wife, Leza Cantoral. He edited the anthologies *Walk Hand in Hand Into Extinction: Stories Inspired by True Detective* and *This Book Ain't Nuttin to Fuck With: A Wu-Tang Tribute Anthology*. He plays bass and sings in the rock band The Dionysus Effect, look out for their debut album in 2021. The follow up to this book will be *Cosplay to the Death* ;)

Spirit Doll of Mandy De Sandra Made by Author
Christine Morgan

Mandy De Sandra is an ancient Gnostic Goddess. She writes Bizarro Erotica, Splatterpunk, political satire, and hardcore horror that has been covered in VICE, Huffington Post, Jezebel, and AV Club. She hates the Demiurge and loves Ray Kurzweil. Kirk Cameron knows she exists and prays to the Demiurge to help her not write anymore naughty books. She will not confirm or deny she dated Alû.

ALSO BY CLASH BOOKS

BURIALS

Jessica Drake-Thomas

HELENA

Claire L. Smith

I'M FROM NOWHERE

Lindsay Lerman

HEXIS

Charlene Elsby

BORN TO BE PUBLIC

Greg Mania

LIFE OF THE PARTY

Tea Hacic

THE MUMMY OF CANAAN

Maxwell Bauman

TRAGEDY QUEENS: STORIES INSPIRED BY LANA DEL REY & SYLVIA PLATH

Edited by Leza Cantoral

GIRL LIKE A BOMB

Autumn Christian

THIS BOOK IS BROUGHT TO YOU BY MY STUDENT LOANS

Megan J. Kaleita

THIS IS A HORROR BOOK

Charles Austin Muir

TRY NOT TO THINK BAD THOUGHTS

Art by Matthew Revert

SEQUELLAND

Jay Slayton-Joslin

JAH HILLS

Unathi Slasha

DARK MOONS RISING IN A STARLESS NIGHT

Mame Bougouma Diene

IF YOU DIED TOMORROW I WOULD EAT YOUR CORPSE

Wrath James White

HORROR FILM POEMS

Poetry by Christoph Paul & Art by Joel Amat Güell

NIGHTMARES IN ECSTASY

Brendan Vidito

50 BARN POEMS

Zac Smith

WE PUT THE LIT IN LITERARY

CLASHBOOKS.COM

FOLLOW US

TWITTER, IG FB

@clashbooks

www.ingramcontent.com/pod-product-compliance
Lightning Source LLC
Chambersburg PA
CBHW032027180726
48284CB00008B/2512